ISLANDS

ISLANDS

© 2018 Writers of Chantilly

ISBN 978-1-970071-00-9

Cover illustration, cover design and book design
©John H. Matthews, www.BookConnectors.com

Edited by S.C. Megale

Published by Bluebullseye Press

ISLANDS

WRITERS OF CHANTILLY

ANTHOLOGY 2018

CONTENTS

INTRODUCTION

After three years as the elected Editor for the Writers of Chantilly (or four? Oh, hell, what did the last anthology say?), and an equal amount of time wrestling with punctuation, prose, and preference with our plethora of diverse and talented writers, it is time a matter of style is addressed.

Some writers prefer towards, while others hope we move towards toward. I hope we're toward towards, lest we go backward or backwards.

There's the matter of commas, where they stay and where they go. Is it theatre or theater? Who really knows?

Whether it's whispered, breathed, sighed, or just hissed, Oxfordian grammar is where I insist.

Every apostrophe knows where its quote should cling. But who's to say for sure which style is king? All apostrophes' dignities are all apostrophes's honor, and with so many choices, really, one wonders, why bother?

There're areas of grey and areas of gray; I've leapt to conclusions I've leaped either way.

On some styles we're consistent, and others we're not. Please remember it's intentional here, because on this literary island, variety is all we've got.

We're a lovable bunch and we've sure got a hunch that we – okay, I swear to God I'm done rhyming.

I just wanted to note that, for at least this volume, we

have relinquished the value of consistency in favor of the value of autonomy for each writer. As Editor, I wanted to make that annotation, but also to say that I look forward always to finding the best ways to work with and help our writers to shine like the lighthouses they are. They bring brightness to me every day.

So chart a course and prepare to cruise the islands we have to offer, laying anchor at each port for a page or six.

We hope you enjoy this fun, evocative, and thoughtful 2018 Anthology. It is an honor to serve and present it.

Editorially,

S.C. Megale
Editor
The Writers of Chantilly

5 DAYS
JOHN H. MATTHEWS

It was into the second day before I noticed the silence. Something had seemed different before that, but I hadn't been able to identify it, to find the source of what was bothering me. The usual sounds were there; birds and bugs, the bellow of Buster the cow wherever she happened to be grazing on the grassy island, chickens doing what chickens do, the waves lapping onto the beach. But still there was a vacuum where there was usually so much more.

I walked my small island from one end to the other, staring at the horizon in each direction. From the west side I could see the shadow low on the water, the mainland. It had been a month, at least, since I last took my boat over to stock up on the supplies I was unable to grow or raise myself. Would be happier with three months, even six.

The solitude my island provided was my savior; the anxiety that had grown inside of me for so many years now tucked away, secured. Occasionally a small boat would pull up on the beach, the occupants ignoring the private property signs, and begin to set up a picnic. Sometimes it was easier to just let them as I watched from afar, the tingle returning ever so slightly to my bones, the nervousness of interacting with others rising to the surface.

There were no boats today, just the silence.

I burned my fire on the beach as always that night, my

unofficial act of lighthouse keeper. The large ships had their charts and navigation, but I always feared a smaller vessel would crash into my island. More sticks were thrown on than usual, sending the flames higher into the air. I watched it burn as the heat enveloped me on that already hot September night. Stars spotted the darkness. I looked for the constellations I knew and noticed the stillness, no movement from above, like the backdrop of a play that was accurate yet lifeless.

The third day I walked the island at least a dozen times, on each lap stopping to train my binoculars on the mainland a few miles away. Nothing. The quiet was growing, invading my every thought, echoing through my head. No boats passed by. No white trail remnants of jet engines streaked across the sky like watercolor brush strokes.

When I woke the next morning in my sleeping bag beside the burned-out fire, the stillness was deafening. After rolling up my makeshift bed and putting it away in the cabin, I walked to the shore facing the mainland and stared. I watched intently for any sign of life, of activity, of normality. Still nothing.

My boat was a small outboard but had plenty of power to make the few mile trip each way when I needed. Its size kept me from bringing anything home I didn't really need, things too large to not be practical for someone living alone on an island. I pulled the tarp off and checked the engine for gas, then gave a pull on the cord. It started on the second try. The sound was startling after the days of silence and I turned it off. Not now, not yet. I knew eventually I'd have to go to shore, to try and find answers, but I couldn't bring myself to do right then. I hoped the silence would end, that everything would be normal again soon, but somewhere inside of me I felt that it would never be normal again.

I slept inside that night and woke after the sun had come up. Light filtered through the blue cotton curtains that hung in my one window. This would be the fifth day of the silence. I knew that I had to go soon, make the trip over to the mainland. Likely I would be proven silly, if not crazy, when I arrived and found everything as it had always been. Cars and trucks, people going about their lives in the coastal town.

Chores were done that needed to be done, eggs retrieved, Buster was milked, solar panels wiped down from the inevitable and unavoidable seagull droppings. I then packed a small bag, locked the cabin door (for what reason I didn't really know) and went to my boat. The tarp was still off and I loaded my bag then pushed it down the sandy beach until the engine would drop into the water.

I felt it before I heard it and froze in place. It got louder as my skin shook from the vibrations. Then the grey fighter jet passed over me, the roar of the engines making me step backward to hold my balance. Just as I thought it was going to be gone, it made a hard turn to the left and came back towards me faster than I thought was possible. It slowed and passed while tilting the left wing down. The pilot's face clearly visible, a young man with dark skin. In that short moment we made eye contact, he smiled and nodded, then looked forward again as he raised a mask to his face. The plane circled back to head its original direction then disappeared.

When the residual whine of the jet was gone, the silence was back. I stared at my boat and then looked out towards the mainland. It wasn't time.

That night I burned the fire taller than it had ever been, stretching a dozen or more feet into the sky. I had no idea what was happening, but did know that someone knew I was here. That thought stayed in my head through dinner and then as I lay down to go to sleep under the stars, wondering if it was a good thing or not. It had happened so fast, the briefest of human interactions, but something about the pilot had calmed me. His smile, his casualness at the controls of an expensive machine of war.

Sleep came and my body soaked it in, dreams moved in and out and the night air cooled around me. I woke with Buster grazing nearby, her tail swatting away the bugs. The morning sky was already blue, then I blinked, closing my eyes tight and opening to look up again.

I jumped up, to get just that much closer to the sky to see better, and I smiled. The white trail stretched across from west to east, disappearing out over the Atlantic. Then I saw another further north. Then another. Running, I grabbed my binoculars from the cabin and went to the western side of the island and looked towards the mainland. All was still at first, then, finally, way over to the left, the slightest reflection of light off the white hull of a boat.

The day was spent watching for boats and counting airplanes and contrails in the sky. It was normal, how it had always been before, but seemed so new and exciting. Buster didn't seem to care no matter how much I talked to her about it.

That night in my cabin I looked at the calendar that hung beside the door. Red lines crisscrossed days that passed on my island, except for the last five where I'd drawn large red question marks. The days had not been normal and didn't deserve to be treated as such.

I took the marker and put a red X on September 16 to end my day.

John H. Matthews is the author of four novels: Family Line, Designated Survivor, The South Coast, *and* Ballyvaughan. *He is a blatant self-promoter of his novels. His proudest accomplishment in life, after the birth of his son, is having a tweet liked by S.E.Hinton. His standards are low. He has a high score of 367 on Crossy Road as of the writing of this bio.*

A GARDEN OF ONE'S OWN
BARBARA OSGOOD

If you have a garden and a library, you have everything you need.

                        - Marcus Tullius Cicero

1939. The black cloud of the Great Depression was giving way to the specter of World War II. I was five years old. We –my mother, father and I—had just moved into a little white house that my father built himself.

It perched at the top of a hill on a dead end road. Only stone walls suggested the land was once a farm. Pastures and plowed fields had been replaced by meadows where goldenrod, Queen Anne's lace, and purple asters grew in waves of color. Butterflies hovered over the flowers. Only the buzzing of the bees penetrated the silence.

The house and the meadows were my world. There were no neighbors. No playmates. There were no excursions to the store or the library. They were miles away. We might as well have been living on an island.

My parents, traumatized by the Depression and the advent of the war, struggled to manage their lives. The daily grind of work and housekeeping exhausted them. I know now that they both suffered from depression. But in the 1940s there was no name for the unseen malady, no pill that would ease their pain.

My father compensated with a frenzy of activity. He turned part of the meadow into a large vegetable garden. I watched while he cultivated the soil, then ran lines of white string to plant straight rows of corn, beans, carrots, beets, radishes, and kale. He assured me that the tiny seeds he had sprinkled in the furrows would soon become vegetables that we could eat. I ran to the garden every morning, looking for plants I had only seen in the pictures on the seed packets.

My mother's energy was at its lowest in the morning. After breakfast she sat at the kitchen table in a trancelike state, smoking, drinking coffee, and playing solitaire. I couldn't penetrate the wall around her. She came alive in the afternoon to resume her household chores, but by then I had wandered off to find other ways to occupy my time.

I learned to be alone.

Books became my companions. Two glass-doored bookcases in the upstairs hall of the house yielded an assortment of titles from my parents' college days: art, mathematics, engineering, botany. One shelf held an outdated set of the *Encyclopedia Britannica*. There were *Outdoor Girls* books from my mother's youth, as well as several Victorian romances from her teenage years.

I curled up on the floor between the bookcases and devoured the printed pages. Understanding them didn't matter. It wasn't the story. It was the act of reading. I was fascinated by words, even if I didn't know what they meant. *Idiosyncratic. Ubiquitous. Antithetical.* They were like music—each with its own melody and cadence. I repeated them over and over in my head. I recited them aloud, savoring the way they rolled from my tongue.

On warm summer days I carried my book to the meadow. No one else knew that there was a large, flat rock hidden in the grass. I lay on the rock, feeling its sun-warmed surface on my back. I watched the butterflies flitting from one flower to another, the bees stopping to collect their pollen. The air was filled with the sweet scent of the flowers and the spicy aroma of the meadow grasses. It was quiet except for that humming of the bees. It was my own personal garden. I delighted in the thought that no one could see me.

*   *   *

In 1941, the war became real. Every night, my parents sat in the living room and listened to the news coming from the big Philco radio in the corner. They said little. But even through my child's eyes I could see that they were worried and afraid.

Our little island in the country became their refuge. Gardening gave respite from the daily onslaught of war news. Digging in the soil relieved the stresses of wartime responsibilities. And seeing plants grow and flourish helped them forget, if only briefly, the destruction that was taking place in another part of the world.

My father expanded his vegetable garden to include asparagus, gooseberries, and currants, enjoying the challenge of growing something different. He planted peanuts to surprise me. Together we watched the plants bloom, then bury shoots in the ground. A few weeks later, when I gasped as I pulled peanuts out of the soil, he chuckled with quiet satisfaction.

My mother's flower garden glowed with riotous color like a botanical oriental rug. She, too, had a surprise for me. A botanist, she could tell me the Latin name for every flower. She grinned with pleasure as she recited names like *Centaurea cyanis, Lobularia maritime,* and my favorite, *Polystichum acrostichoides,* the Christmas fern. I begged her to repeat it over and over: *Polystichum acrostichoides.*

There was music in the lyrical plant names. I had found amazing words in my books. But there were even more amazing words in my mother's garden.

* * *

At Christmas that year, there was a new book under the tree. *The Secret Garden.* I pulled the wrapping away and began to read.

When Mary Lennox was sent to Misselthwaite Manor to live with her uncle, everybody said she was the most disagreeable looking child ever seen…"

I didn't stop reading until I reached the last page.

I was part of the story. I felt Mary's loneliness. I turned the key in the rusty gate and saw the deserted garden.

In the past I had only read words. *The Secret Garden* brought the words to life. It stirred me as no other book had done. It was like the first taste of a delicious, exotic fruit.

I have read many books since that childhood encounter. Academic books. Fiction. Books with messages. Funny books. But *The Secret Garden* claims a special place in my memory. Even today, so many years later, I wonder what it would be like to live in a big house where there are rooms I have never seen. Where there is a garden gate waiting to be opened.

*   *   *

Gardens have been my refuge since those desolate days of World War II. When I was all alone, I found solace in the quiet order of my father's vegetable garden, the peace and sensual beauty of the meadow, the mystery of the fictional secret garden.

I till my own garden now. It is full of memories. I grow colorful flowers there. And a *Polystichum acrostichoides.*

Barbara Osgood is a native New Yorker who earned her PhD in Human Ecology from Cornell University. She retired as a senior executive from the Natural Resources Conservation Service, U.S. Department of Agriculture in 2002. Her passion is rescuing old Labrador Retrievers, but at age 83 she now has a new passion: creative writing. She lives and writes at home in Fairfax, Virginia, with two old Labs, Molly and Benji.

AN EXTRAORDINARY, ORDINARY MAN
DIANE HUNTER

It's not how my brother died, but how he lived with Stage Four cancer for four years that's impacted me the most. Bob was seventy-two when he passed away on April 29, 2008, and he left behind the legacy of a life well-lived as an ordinary man.

I was the youngest of three. My sister, Dolores, left home when she was seventeen. I was six at the time. Bob was ten. Growing up in the 1940s was different. No TV. We had to entertain ourselves, especially during summer vacation.

Bob and I were opposites. I was the noisy, pesky tag-a-long little sister. He was the laid back, reserved big brother who tolerated me. Even though he was on the quiet side, he had a sneaky, subtle sense of humor that could attack in an instant and retreat before anyone knew what happened. Occasionally we teamed up to get what we wanted, like the time we talked our parents into keeping an abandoned puppy. We played Monopoly when his friends weren't available. In the end, we usually fought over something *I did wrong*. On a day to day basis, we went our separate ways.

As we grew older, the differences between us became more obvious. In school, I wanted to be a part of everything. Bob wasn't a joiner. He had a select group of friends that he was comfortable with, but he also enjoyed his alone time.

Around the house, he kept to himself, except when he was taunting me.

I was twelve when Mom took us to Silverman's Department Store for going-back-to-school clothes. To my dismay, I found myself in the "Chubette" section. My love of chocolate milkshakes helped me to blossom into a plumpish pre-teen. The transformation hadn't gone unnoticed by my lean and mean brother. It garnered his full attention. At home, he heckled me without mercy.

When Mom left the room, he slid next to me and whispered, "You are now the Big F.

He thought that was funnier than saying, "Fat."

I yelled for help. "Mom, Bob just called me a name!"

"Bob, cut it out. Tell her you're sorry."

"Okay." He still had a smirk on his face as he apologized. "Sorry, Effie." Another insulting nickname!

"Mom, he did it again!" Bob disappeared.

Revenge was mine—one time. My big bro loved to construct things. It took him two months to build a row boat. Why he decided to build it in the basement is unknown. When he finished, he asked a neighbor to help him carry it outside. They hoisted it up the stairs to a side door, but there wasn't room to turn it and get it through. Bob had to dismantle it and rebuild it in the yard. Once this was done, he headed to the Allegheny River for the launch. It took only minutes to sink! He was devastated. I wanted to feel sorry for him, but my sympathy was short-lived. I waited for his frustration to peak. It was a delightful moment when I gave him a "Na-na na na-na" payback.

My self-image crashed for the next two years. It wasn't

only because of my brother's heckling. Everything about me felt awkward. I avoided looking in the mirror. When I turned fourteen, my fairy godmother must have waved her magic wand because "Effie" disappeared. In her place was a svelte me. The teasing stopped. Now, we didn't talk at all, but it didn't matter because Bob was off to Penn State University. For a while, it was nice to be an only child. After two years, he decided to leave State to find a job. We had to deal with the uncomfortable situation of being together at home. Then, I left for Grove City College. At the beginning of the second semester, our father died of cancer. I continued for three more semesters, but Mom was struggling financially. Leaving school to find a job seemed liked the right thing to do.

I got a job as a secretary in downtown Pittsburgh and started night school at Duquesne University. Even though Bob and I lived under the same roof, we didn't encroach on each other's privacy. There were times we would pass each other going up and down the stairs. We were careful not to brush shoulders. I think each of us thought the other one didn't care. Traveling back and forth became tiresome, so I eventually rented an apartment with a friend. Bob also left home for an apartment close to the University of Pittsburg where he was completing his degree. Aside from Mom telling me this, I would have had no idea of where he was or what he was doing. Life had a surprise in store for me.

One evening, my phone rang.

"Hello."

"Diane, this is Bob."

Long pause. "Bob who?"

Nervous laugh. "Your brother."

My brother—calling me?

"Bet you're surprised, huh?"

Surprised? Oh my God, something must have happened. "What's wrong?"

Nervous laugh again. "Nothing. Sorry if I scared you. I was wondering if you could come home this weekend. There's someone special I'd like you to meet."

Someone special? Is he asking me to meet a girlfriend?

"Uh,yeah. Sure. I guess I can. Well, yes, I'll come home this weekend."

"Okay, see you then." *Am I dreaming? Did this just happen? I need to call Mom.*

"Hello."

"Mom, guess who called me a few minutes ago?"

"Bob."

"Did you tell him to?"

"No, he called to ask for your number." I could hear her smiling.

"What's going on? He asked me to come home to meet someone. Is this about a girl?"

"Oh, it's more than that. I think they're talking about marriage. Her name is Carol. She's from Vermont and a student at Mt. Mercy College. Her roommate is dating Bob's friend. That's how they met. Carol is very pretty and sweet as can be. I liked her immediately. You will too."

I could tell by Mom's voice that she was happy. My first reaction to this news was that maybe things could change for Bob and me. To include me seemed like an olive branch, an invitation to be present in his future. When Saturday came, I hopped on a bus for an hour-long ride home. When I arrived, everyone was in the kitchen. Receiving a genuine smile from my brother was an ice breaker!

Bob was a little awkward with the introduction. "Uh, Diane, this is Carol." He was blushing. He looked like a guy in love.

Carol and I were comfortable with each other from the start.

"I've been looking forward to meeting you. Bob told me all about you and some funny stories about when you were kids."

Really? Wonder if he told her about Effie? Bob looked like he had too much starch in his collar. He was uneasy.

Maybe he thinks I'll tell on him. I had a long rap sheet.

We enjoyed a lot of girl talk. I could tell from her body language this wasn't a casual relationship. She was rock solid. Mom was right about her. My brother had chosen well. From that moment on, a friendship was born. Not long after this first meeting, we met again. She asked me to be a bridesmaid for their October 13 wedding in her hometown of Randolph Center, Vermont.

The day of their wedding was one of the most beautiful autumn days one would expect in a New England setting. The ceremony was lovely. I was honored to be part of it. I had never seen Bob so happy. He and I talked as though we liked each other. Well, we did—I think. It was something new, so I was hoping it wasn't just for the occasion. After their wedding, they settled in Washington, D.C. Bob worked for the Army Map Service. There wasn't a chance we would see each other except for holidays, but a chapter in our lives had turned a page. We were grownups now and had a chance to start over again.

A year after their wedding, they welcomed a beautiful daughter, Kim. When they came home to visit, I was there enjoying time with them. Carol brought warmth into our family. I regarded her as a sister. To this day, I credit her with the change in Bob that brought us together.

In 1964, I visited them in D.C. I spent my time sightseeing, but I had something else in mind after being in the city a few days. I wanted to see what employment opportunities were available. Capitol Hill intrigued me. Maybe I could find a job with a Senator or Congressman. I stopped by an employment agency, filled out an application, and got to know the owner and her assistant, Joanne. Jo found me a job in an instant. Her roommate had gotten married. She asked if I would like to share her apartment until I got settled. When I told this to Bob and Carol, they were very supportive. I had confided in them several times about feeling like I was treading water and needed to make some changes. I decided to make the move. A few days before Memorial Day, I said goodbye to Pittsburgh and hello to the District of Columbia. On the holiday, I went to Chesapeake Beach for the day. There, I met Reuben Hunter. Seven months later, we were married. He was serving in the Air Force in Anchorage, Alaska. After three years, we could have settled anywhere upon his discharge, but chose to go back to D.C. to be near Bob and Carol.

We lived a few blocks from each other in Sterling, Virginia. They now had an adorable daughter, Kristen. On New Year's Eve 1968, the four of us celebrated at a Knights of Columbus party. Bob surprised me again.

"Would you like to dance?" I must have looked shocked. "I guess it's okay if I ask my sister for a dance." He said this with his trademark nervous laugh. It was awkward for both of us. Even more unexpected was the stroke of midnight. He came over to hug me.

"Happy New Year."

"Happy New Year, Bob." I blurted out, "I love you." It became one of those *what do I say* moments for him, but he smiled.

"I love you too." We had crossed another threshold.

In March 1969, Bob and Carol had a son, Scott. Nine months later, we welcomed our first son, Gregg. In October 1973, we completed our family with our son, Chris. Our families were close. Bob and Reuben regarded each other as brothers. The cousins spent a lot of time together. Uncle Bob was a role model. This was a dream come true for me. Life was good.

In the early 1980s, Reuben and I started a tradition with Bob's family and some friends that continues today—our Christmas Eve supper. It was a get-together to celebrate the ending of one year and the beginning of another. For me, it meant something more. I regretted all the Christmases that Bob and I never spoke, never gave each other a nod or a gift. This supper represented a healing and became a gift we could enjoy together with people we loved.

My brother wasn't perfect. He had a dark side. It revealed itself at the beginning of the Notre Dame Football season. He was rabid about his team. When they won, his world was serene. If they lost, he would sulk for days without the benefit of company. Not one to make waves, it surprised us when he gave a strong response to an editorial about Notre Dame on the sports page of the Washington Post. There was a controversy about who should be named as National Champions—Notre Dame or University of Miami. The title was given to Miami. Along with many others, Bob strongly defended the winning record of his adopted alma mater.

In 1991, I decided to go back to work full time. I was fortunate to land a job in the same social services office where Carol worked. This brought us even closer. Bob had taken an early retirement and was enjoying being away from the rat race. He's the only one I've ever known who thought retiring was a beginning, not an ending. Not being driven by his or anyone's agenda gave him the private time he needed. He enjoyed a leisure cup of coffee at Starbucks, a day of browsing at Home Depot or puttering around his garage/machine shop. His joy was another man's boredom, but this is what everyone loved about him. He wasn't caught up in the world. This freed him to sit, talk, and most of all, listen.

Bob also gave time to his community. For five years he assisted in driving patients to their doctors' appointments. He had taken a gentleman to his dialysis treatments a number of times. Their friendship became a human interest story that appeared in the Loudoun Times Mirror, along with a photo of them. It was typical of Bob to not talk about acts of kindness. I wasn't aware until years later that he had done this, but not surprised. He didn't bring attention to himself.

I remember the day in 1992 when Carol came to my desk at the office. She was upset.

"We just found out that Bob has kidney cancer."

I was stunned. "How bad is it?"

"He has to have surgery. They're going to remove the kidney."

Both of our parents had suffered from cancer for two years. It changed our lives. I was sick with worry about what lay ahead for Bob. Dad and I weren't close. He died when I was nineteen. What I had missed with him, I had found with Bob. I called him when I got home from work.

"Carol told me what happened. Do you feel like talking?"

He paused, cleared his throat. "Well, there's not much to talk about. I won't know anything until after the surgery."

I wanted to ask questions, but knew better. A lot of what Bob felt stayed inside. This was characteristic of him. I told him I loved him.

"I love you too." That was the extent of our conversation.

Carol called me after his surgery. The doctor was confident that the cancer hadn't spread. As time passed, all seemed well. Our lives got back to normal.

*   *   *

Twelve years passed. While on vacation in Ocean City, Maryland, Bob fell ill. The ER doctor found something concerning on an X-ray. The cancer had returned. It was Stage 4. He called me.

"Guess you heard."

"What do you plan to do?"

"According to the doctors, it's too advanced. No treatment will stop it from spreading." There was a resolve in his voice that kept me from breaking down. I thought about the pain this would bring to Carol, their children, and their grandchildren. Bob was enjoying life. No one could fathom him not being here with us.

"Whatever you need us to do, we'll be there for you. We'll stay close to Carol."

"Thanks. I know you will."

My next question was inevitable. Bob must have known because he offered an answer before I asked.

"I don't know how much time I have. That will depend on how rapidly it progresses. I'll be tested every three months. Right now, I'm okay."

"I'm gonna pray for a miracle, Bob."

"I think it will take one."

This was the beginning of a journey that none of us could have predicted. Instead of retreating from life, Bob kept moving forward. He set a pace. Holidays became even more special. Carol never had to plead with him to decorate. This was his specialty. His spirits were high, as though nothing was going on. When the results came back from his first PET test, he made sure I knew.

"Nothing has changed the past few months. I'm still feeling good."

Thank God. We can breathe for a while longer.

I don't know what Bob's innermost thoughts were. This hung over him for the next three years. I'm sure the fear of the future was always present for him, but he didn't display this to anyone. I never saw him waver. He fought hard in his own way by living each day as he chose. We celebrated his seventieth birthday with a bash at a local restaurant. Our families celebrated on Thanksgiving, Christmas, and special occasions. Because of his calmness, we were able to go about our daily activities. Carol and their children exhibited the same strength as Bob. They followed his lead. We followed theirs. But time was running out.

In July 2007, Bob showed signs of slowing down. He had a talk with Reuben.

"I can tell a difference. My last test showed the cancer progressing. I can't complain. I've been able to do everything I wanted to do." When he spoke with me on the phone about the change, I broke down. He understood.

"Diane, don't worry. It will all work out the way it should."

Christmas Eve supper 2007 had a different feeling to it. I could see the change in him. He smiled less, even though he kept to the spirit of the evening. My heart was breaking because I knew it would be the last time we would be together for the holidays. By the time Spring arrived, he was homebound. I started taking extended lunch breaks to visit with him. He liked to sit in his favorite recliner in the den. We talked about a wide range of things – childhood memories, "Effie," Notre Dame, and favorite foods. We talked about God and our faith. Not once did we talk about dying. I knew he had decided to have hospice care at home. Being in the hospital was not an option.

Reuben accompanied me on one of my lunchtime visits. It was difficult for him because he was an only child, and Bob had been like his brother. They were fishing buddies.

As we readied to leave, Reuben offered a hug and burst into tears. Bob raised himself up from his chair and wept with him. It was the first time I had seen my brother cry. I joined. Carol walked into the room and saw us huddled together. She put the moment in perspective.

"I think a good cry is just what we need." It was a way of letting go.

A few days later, I came back. This time Bob wasn't in his chair. He was in bed. When I brushed my hand against his foot to let him know I was there, he opened his eyes, but didn't move. His voice was barely audible.

"Too weak."

"Are you in pain?"

"No."

"I'll come back another day when you're up to having company." I paused. "I love you."

"I love you too." These were the last words we spoke to each other.

English poet John Donne wrote, "No man is an island, entire of itself. Every man is a piece of the continent, a part of the main." I think of an island as remote, hard to get to, but it offers an escape. Its lack of connectivity draws people to it in the hope of finding peace and tranquility. It offers privacy. Insignificant as it may be to the land mass around it, an island is still a part of the main. Bob loved his time alone, but he was also a part of the main. He had a heart that overflowed to those he loved and who needed him. There was never a conflict of interest. This is what drew all of us to him.

Bob died at home surrounded by family. He did "go gentle

into that good night." When we gathered in the evening to talk about arrangements, we felt at peace. At his funeral, his daughter, Kristen, and daughter-in-law, Annalea, delivered a beautiful tribute. I also spoke. Here are excerpts from my remarks:

Bob was our safety net. He was a quiet man with a gentle heart that knew how to give to each person what they needed most. He asked for nothing in return. I will remember him for his subtle humor and his caring, for his common-sense logic that helped calm many a storm, for his genuine love that was never pretentious or overbearing, for his acts of kindness that defined his character and beliefs. Bob took time to smell the roses all of his life. He didn't live for the pursuit of wealth or recognition. All the things that most of us consider mundane and routine, he appreciated and found joy in. These past four years have been remarkable. He faced every day not knowing when he would be overtaken by the cancer, and he did it with amazing grace. He never lived in denial or made us bear his burden. He let us walk along with him. We walked with him as far as we could—he went the rest of the way by himself. The disease had robbed him of his earthly life; it couldn't rob him of his eternal one. During one of my last conversations with him, I said he was a hero. He didn't accept that. To him a hero was a great person who made a name for himself in the eyes of the world. But a hero is also someone who does the right things when no one is looking. That was my brother. He lived his life completely and left us better and stronger for having known him. He truly was an extraordinary, ordinary man.

DIANE HUNTER lives in Herndon, Virginia with her husband of 53 years, Reuben. She has been a member of Writers of Chantilly since 2004, contributing each year to our anthologies with a purpose. She is compiling a personal and family history with each story to pass on to future generations.

DONNE AND DONE
PATRICIA BOSWELL KALLMAN

"No man is an island," we've all read.
Truer words, we agree, have never been said.
Why is this line unequivocally sound?
What thoughts lead to this pronouncement profound?

If not an island, then what are we?
What topography makes you you and me me?
We are dirt; we are rock; we are gold to be panned.
We nourish, support, and we shift like the sands.

Foundation of continents under us deep,
We erupt like volcanos; like lava we creep
From the depths of the caves to the steppes as we seek,
We rise to the hills, to the highest of peaks.

Peninsulas, we jut out and away.
But locked to the land, aground we stay.
Though islands beckon, we stand on the moor.
Wholly ingrained, we are stranded ashore.

HAWAIIAN WAVES
PATRICIA BOSWELL KALLMAN

A fuse of foam leaves nightfall in its wake.
A ghostly chorus line enters
Dancing precisely in the dark
Followed by another,
And another.
They will dance until all is black; then they will still be
heard.
May I dance like these until all is black, and may my voice
still be heard.

PATRICIA BOSWELL KALLMAN is an award-winning writer, director, and producer in theatre and television. She is a co-founder of The Alliance Theatre in Virginia. Pat and husband, Roy, are proud parents of two daughters.

ISLANDS
S.C. MEGALE

This poem is dedicated to my 6th grade English teacher, Mrs. Anderson. It has absolutely nothing to do with her. One day I arrived to her class and totally forgot it was Poem Day. Freaking Poem Day! All we had to do was pick any poem and read it. ANY DAMN POEM. The boy to my right read SPONGEBOB LYRICS. I had nothing. I, in a tiny, humiliation-ridden voice, only said, "I forgot it was Poem Day" when my name was called. The lip pucker and disappointed, deep eyes of Mrs. Anderson followed by a little "Hmm" haunted my pride for years as I was quickly discarded and attentions moved on to the next student poet. I hung my head in the circle of shame – mean, desks. I asked not for a make-up assignment or the opportunity to turn it in late. I accepted my fate and vowed then to make it up to dear Mrs. Anderson somehow. Years passed as I plotted my return to grace. I attended her son's wedding, danced and ate, all the while wondering, behind her sparkling earrings and overjoyed smile, "Does she remember Poem Day?" Is she thinking of Poem Day RIGHT NOW as she is clapping for the Best Man's speech? What if HE had forgotten Speech Day? Would there be a disappointed pucker? Does Poem Day haunt her in the shadows of her bed covers too? Does Poem Day stir up questions of what if, or how could it have been? I will receive no grade for this, but finally, at last, it is here. My redemption. My second chance. Mrs. Anderson, not only do I present you with a poem, but it is a poem dedicated to YOU! Yes, YOU! Mrs. Mary Evelyn Anderson. This is your poem given to you with my love and my apologies. May Poem Day be avenged. May justice reign. May my honor be restored on this day.

TL/DR: Mrs. Anderson, this one's for you.

Caught between fire and water are we
Harden like lava and tether the sea
Like balls on a chain
We're dragged through the grain
What great crumbling mountains we'd be

But I am not nearly like you
You're six-foot-a-million, I'm two
You're fish and I'm crab
You're laughing I'm mad
Out of cerulean and aqua you're blue

So countries load cannons with these
They rumble the grid lines and keys
At our steps the grounds crack
It's a tightrope we lack
And differences again bloody knees

Islands of ourselves do we make
Closing our ports in each wake
I'd be a little white speck
Under the U in Quebec
And you'd be the vowel in lake

S.C. MEGALE did not get any sleep last night, so this bio is really short. She was born in 1995 and is the author of fourteen Young Adult novels, including her upcoming publication with St. Martin's Press, This is Not a Love Scene. *Goodnight.*

ISLAND GIRL
ANGIE CARRERA

The minute I see her, I know she's going to be trouble.

She's been escorted into my office along with another girl, and without so much as a glance my way, she strides past us all. She plants herself on a solitary chair across the room, a good fifteen feet from my desk. I haven't even gotten a glimpse of her face before feeling her energy, dark and menacing.

Mrs. McGee, the teacher of our internal alternative high school, introduces me to the girls, both age sixteen, which means they would be good candidates for one of the fine volunteers from our mentoring program.

Amy, a petite blonde, reminds me of a popular cheerleader from my high school days. After answering a few basic questions about how she came to be court-involved, she expresses her desire to get a mentor to sponsor her in a twelve-step program for teens so she can get out of probation. When she feels that she's impressed me sufficiently, the girl smiles broadly, agreeing to provide the required program application by the next morning.

Mrs. McGee hands me the girl's file and excuses her. I have a distinct feeling I'll never see the promised application. I'll do the routine follow-up but don't hold out much hope. After two years of running this program, I've developed a sense of who will take advantage of the program and who won't.

Now for the dark-haired girl.

My eyes move across the room along the gray floor tiles until they come to rest on what I can only describe as shit-kicker boots.

The girl sits slouched forward, one elbow on each knee, letting gravity pull a ragged curtain of hair over her face down to her nose. With knees apart in blue jeans that hang long and loose, she sports a dark plaid shirt which she wears with the authority of a tribal chieftain. She seems to have drawn a circle around herself, an island. She is its ruler.

Mrs. McGee looks decidedly uncomfortable. "Krista is in court school because of aggressive behavior in her regular school. Her behavior hasn't improved and she's in danger of being expelled from this alternative program as well." She hands me the girl's file and a note from her probation officer supporting Mrs. McGee's belief that a mentor might help with Krista's behavior both in and out of school.

Her file contains notes from teachers and intake workers, mostly indicating frustration with a teen who seems both spirits and smart. I glance through the school records which, until her first encounter with the court as a fourteen year old runaway, had shown exceptional grades but right now are pretty dismal.

I see Krista eyeing me from under the hair. When she sees me looking at her, she glares, daring me to be a well-meaning but stupid adult.

Her message is clear. *Do NOT expect me to participate.* Her jaw, what I can see of it, is set grimly in the afternoon light. She looks scary, and her file tells me she *is* as scary as she looks.

"Krista," I say, indicating a very comfortable chair near my desk, "would you like to move over here? You might be more comfortable."

"No, thanks, I'm fine right here." She does not look up.

So that's how it's going to be. I decide to go on the offensive. Leaning back in my chair and with the air of someone remarking on travel plans, I say, "Alright, Krista. So what do you plan to do after you graduate from college?"

Her eyebrows rise at the question. She probably assumed I would ask the same questions I had of the other girl. Instead, I decide to cut to the chase. Let's see if I can get her to step off the island, at least long enough to get her into my mentoring program.

After a moment's rebound, she squints at me, then at the teacher. I can hear her thinking. Did I really mean to ask that particular question, or had she misheard it? Turning back to me, she snarls, "You wouldn't understand." I feel an intake of breath from Mrs. McGee. I pray she won't interject with a prompt or chastisement. Thankfully, she seems thunderstruck by both my question and Krista's response.

There is something about this girl. Whatever it is, she certainly knows how to command attention. All I needs is one response to prove me right about what I sense is hidden behind the powerful energy she emits.

I take a breath, smile and lean forward. "If I don't understand, I'll definitely let you know. So why don't you just tell me and we can take it from there?"

She grunts and throws her remark clear across the room like a baseball that she just knows I will miss. "I want to help gang members in L.A."

Not to be dissuaded, I challenge her to explain. Let's see where she goes with this. "What do you mean 'help gang members'? Do you intend to help them hold up liquor stores, beat up old ladies, what….?"

She smirks or smiles, I'm not sure which. Then her countenance grows serious and she faces me head on, moving her hair out of her eyes. It is then I see a face full of anger and frustration. A Latina face. A beautiful face on someone who does not know she is beautiful. As a Latina myself, I wonder from what part of the world she or her parents had immigrated.

"No, I want to help them have, you know, better lives."

At this point, I hear the teacher shift ever so slightly forward in her seat, preparing to make corrections to what is, to her, clearly a contrivance. I match the girl's look, deciding to go for broke.

"Krista, I can tell you're a leader-type," I pronounce, sounding a lot like Alex Trebek announcing a Jeopardy winner. Mrs. McGee turns in her seat, ready to tell me I have it all wrong. Krista just stares.

I drag out a "Soooooo…" with my brain scrambling to find the right thing to say.

Then it comes to me.

"If you want, and your parents and teacher agree, I'm inviting you to come with me to a leadership seminar I am teaching in DC next Thursday morning."

Her look goes from confused to stunned.

I keep going. "If you accept this invitation, you'll accompany me to this three-hour seminar and act as my assistant, helping attendees fill out the sign-up sheet, telling them where the restrooms are, and passing out materials. The attendees are female college students, some just a bit older than you."

For a minute I think Mrs. McGee might have fainted but instead, she sits frozen in her chair as if her world is spinning out of control. Until now, the girl has refused all other services and considers court staff her enemies. I move on.

"You'll listen to the seminar and take notes. Afterwards, you and I will talk about what you learned and how you might use your skills to help gang members. What do you think?"

She looks straight at me as if challenging me to take back the invitation. Then, there it is, in the air, the one word I am waiting for.

"Okay."

I turn to Mrs. McGee. In the face of Krista's acquiescence, she can only respond, "Y-yes, that can be arranged." As I watch her scribble out a permission slip excusing Krista from class for the appointed day, I realize that despite any concern that Krista could bolt during our outing, Mrs. McGee might be more than a little relieved to have the girl out of her classroom. An opportunity not to be missed!

I turn back to Krista.

"Krista, for you to come with me, I will need a note from your parents or guardian giving permission for you to travel with me to the seminar. It has to be on my desk by 4:00 P.M. tomorrow. Can you do that?"

I hold out my business card indicating my court title and

contact information. She strides over to accept it, glances at it, and then takes her seat again across the room. I have to smile. She's making it clear that she has not given into anything. She's still in charge of her island.

"Yeah, I can."

"I'll pick you up from your home at 7:45 A.M. on Thursday and you must be ready. I cannot be late. If you're not ready, I may have to leave without you. Do you understand?"

"Yeah, I understand."

"Please let your parents know that we will probably be back in Virginia around 2:30 P.M. if we stop for lunch. You'll remain in my charge until I drop you back to your classroom or home. Otherwise all bets are off. Understood?"

"Understood." This time, she does a short salute and then, catching herself, she looks down.

"And, Krista, be sure your home address is written on the permission note and that it's legible, okay?"

"Okay."

So far she has spoken less than forty words the entire visit, but I'm hopeful that a conversation on the ride in will elicit information that can help me place her with the right mentor.

Mrs. McGee suggests that it would be best for me to take Krista home directly if we stop for lunch because school will be ending by time we get back to the area. Thanking me for my time, she escorts Krista back to the classroom on the lower level.

I sit wondering about the energy left behind by that dark-haired girl.

The next morning, I'm not surprised that the application for the petite blonde student is not waiting for me. However, there shoved under my door I find the parental permission for Krista, along with a neatly printed home address. Now I'm faced with determining exactly how I am going to secure a successful enrollment from this troubled teen that can certainly benefit from all the program has to offer.

On Thursday, I arrive in Krista's neighborhood, with is surprisingly close to the courthouse. I'm a few minutes early since I want to make sure that a parent really knows about the trip. The morning sun does little to brighten the street with its neglected yards and overcast gloom. The house number directs me to a small two-story townhouse painted beige like its neighbors. Although Krista's front yard is well kept, I feel a deep sense of sadness as I approach the doorway. I knock.

"Yes?" says a woman, most likely Krista's mother, answering the door. If she's Krista's mom, my fleeting peek at her says that her daughter has inherited most of her looks from her mother.

"Hello, my name is Angela DeCristofaro from Juvenile Court and I'm here to pick up Krista to –"

The mom doesn't seem interested in talking. She leaves me standing at the open door. Instead, she yells for Krista to "Come down for the lady!" as she heads down the dark hallway back to the interior rooms of the house.

In less than a minute, Krista comes bounding down the steps and, seeing me waiting at the door, opens it wider for me to step inside as she greets me. She looks at my business suit and hesitates before asking, "Do I look okay?" She looks well-groomed with her hair pulled back into a low pony tail. She is dressed in a pair of black pants and proper shoes. She wears no makeup, but frankly, she does not need any.

"The only problem is your tank top. Do you have a jacket to wear on top of it?"

"A jean jacket is all I have but it's not here. I lent it to my friend."

"Well, the tank top will not do. How about a blouse or any top that you would wear to a special place or to church?"

She frowns but then brightens. "I'll be right back, okay?"

A minute later, she returns in a white blouse with short sleeves – a wise choice.

We're off! I'm glad I had insisted on an early start, because I soon find that Krista has not eaten breakfast. A stop at a fast-food drive-through is now in order.

"Krista, I noticed in your file that your birth name is Christina," I say as we unwrap breakfast sandwiches. "I thought your nickname would be Tina."

Her face registers distaste. "I like Krista better. Besides, everyone's used to it. None of my friends would dare call me Christina or Tina." Her shoulders tense, anticipating an argument from me.

Now I understand. On her, *Tina* wouldn't have the authority of *Krista*, so I offer, "Well, my name in Spanish is really long so I go by Angela to make it easier for everyone. But you can call me Angie."

"Okay. I wasn't really sure what to call you." Her shoulders ease and she bites into her breakfast sandwich.

Minutes later, my Saturn is headed down the highway for

the long ride into DC.

"Just so I don't forget, let's go over what I expect of you at the workshop. In one box that we carry in, there are name tags and markers along with sign-in sheets, folders, and other supplies. You'll be sitting near the door at the registration table. Attendees will enter and you'll ask them to sign in and make their own name tags. Remind each of them to pick up a folder with material for them to use during the workshop.   Please be sure that every attendee signs in, even if they come late."

I look over to see if she is paying attention. She seems to be.

"Your job will be easier if you're pleasant to folks as they arrive. You can say something like, 'Good morning. Please sign-in and then take a folder from the table. You can make yourself a name tag with the marker and tags over there.'" I pause. "Can you do that?"

"Yeah, I can do that."

I fix my eyes back on the road and continue.

"While you set up the registration table, I'll be setting up the audio-visual equipment for the PowerPoint presentation. However, you can let me know if you run into any problems."

"Okay."

"I also expect you to help clean up before we leave. I have a policy that I always leave a place better than I found it. This means we must clear the room and tables of all trash and put any movable furniture where it was before we came."

"Sure."

"Oh, and Krista – I want to thank you for agreeing to help me out."

She gives me an odd look and then stares out the window. Then not another word for the rest of the ride.

Soon we arrive at the inside parking lot. Krista offers to carry materials into the training room so I let her. Once at the registration table, she seems a little quieter than I expect, but I soon see her doing an adequate job of greeting guests, handing out materials, having everyone sign in and make name badges.

The class has fourteen young women taking it as a leadership elective. They're smart and interested so the class is off to a good start.

I'm pleased to see Krista color a little when I introduce her to the attendees as my assistant. Although I don't see her taking notes, she performs her other tasks as required. I make a mental note to ask her what she thought of the class, the students, and the day as a whole. This could prove to be a most interesting lunch conversation.

Moving up and down between the desks to make a point, it strikes me that despite their ages and backgrounds, none of these young ladies exude the dynamic energy that I saw in Krista the day I met her. But now she seems so quiet and reserved. Had I been mistaken?

The room is soon filled with chatter and it delights me that the attendees express dismay as I end the session. Krista and I pack up the seminar evaluations and close the room. We are on our way to the car when my stomach growls.

"I must be hungry!" I remark, "How about you?"

"Yeah, I'm starving."

I drive us to Casa Italia, my favorite restaurant, for lunch and we sit in peaceful silence as Krista peruses the menu. I order my regular lasagna with garlic bread and, instead of picking something from the menu, Krista orders the same.

"Are you sure that's what you want? There are lots of good choices."

"Yeah, it's okay. I never had any of this stuff."

"Okay, then do try the lasagna. I'm sure you'll like it. What kind of food are you used to?"

"Mostly I eat whatever is around the house. My mom's always working or out. But when she's home, she makes great dishes with chorizo."

"Where is your family from?"

"My mom's from Paraguay. My dad is from Brazil."

So that accounts for that beautiful face! I wonder what accounts for that flash of anger I witnessed before.

"So it is just your mom and you still at home?"

"No, my brothers too."

"Older or younger?"

"Younger. I keep an eye on them when Mom's not around."

The waitress drops off two glasses of water and says she'll be back with the garlic bread.

"Krista, how did you like going into DC?"

"Oh, I've been to DC before."

"Really? When were you in DC?"

"Uh, it was a while back, with some friends." She looks up at the waitress and the large tray carrying our garlic bread and someone else's meals.

Realizing I may have put her on the spot, I remark, "Well,

I grew up in DC. My mom and I came here from Ecuador when I was a toddler, so I consider DC my hometown. I have a sister who lives nearby and a brother who's in the military. I have a cat." I pause to see how she'll respond, or if she'll tell me something about herself.

"I like cats," she notes, and tears apart her garlic bread. I wait in silence.

The waitress reappears with the lasagna. I say, "Let me know how you like the food. I absolutely love this lasagna. That's why I come here… for the lasagna."

Krista begins cutting her pasta. "Cool."

We eat quietly for a while. Then, covering her mouth politely, she asks if I have read all her files.

"So far, only the part relates to your probation. It's part of my job to know what's going on with each of the mentees so that I can properly match them to a good mentor."

"So what is a mentor really?" She cuts more lasagna.

"An adult friend who listens to you and helps you develop something calls 'discernment'."

"What's that?"

"The dictionary would probably say something like 'A clear understanding of things' but to me, it means more than that. It means being able to fully recognize the events and behaviors of people around us. This helps all of us, kids and adults, make better decisions and guides us in our reactions to those events or people, especially when things are confusing or emotions are high."

"Oh, yeah. I get it."

I am not sure if she did get it or if she just wants to eat her meal.

"Here's an example…" I wait to see if she's going to roll her eyes or look away. Instead she looks attentive.

"Let's say that you make a new friend. She's really cool and has cool friends. She has nice things and knows how to have fun. Most of all, she is interested in knowing all about you. So you hang out with her. Then one day, you're both hanging out and she starts talking about a girl who used to be her friend. She tells you stuff about the girl. Some of the stuff seems private, like an abortion or STD."

Krista looks at me, not understanding.

"'Discernment' is figuring out that if the new friend is comfortable sharing other people's private information, she will probably be comfortable sharing your private information too. What happens if you're not friends anymore? Or if you just lose touch? Will she honor your need for confidentiality?"

Krista nods and says, "Yeah, I know some girls like that from my old high school, talking behind your back or making up sh…." Stopping mid-word, she changes course. "…or making up stuff!"

We both take big forkfuls of lasagna into our mouths. When we see each other with red sauce dripping from our chins, we both grin and reach for napkins.

I tell her, "I have been very lucky to have good people who were kind of like mentors to me."

"Yeah, why did you need a mentor? Were you in trouble too?"

"No, but everyone can benefit from a mentor. My mentors helped me realize my potential. The person I match you with will do that for you, if you let her. Also this person will respect you and your privacy. That is, anything you tell them will be strictly confidential, with only two exceptions."

She looks up from her plate. "Like what?"

"Anything you say or do that leads the mentor to believe you will hurt yourself or hurt others. Your mentor will care about your safety and wellbeing so she'll do everything in her power to protect you so if you indicate that you are in danger of hurting yourself or others, she is obligated to tell someone. Just like you would to protect your brothers. That makes sense, doesn't it?"

She considers this. "Yeah, I guess so…"

"Krista, tell me about what you'd like to have in a mentor?"

She isn't sure, but replies, "Can I think about it and get back to you?" I have to hide my smile, thinking *what a businesslike thing to say.*

Then I begin gently asking her more questions about herself and her family. This is information I can use to match her with the right mentor.

As the smells of garlic bread and delicious lasagna waft around us, Krista opens up about her brothers and things at home which, like some of the other worrisome stories I had heard during my years at court, confirms what I have read in her file. I even find out that we have a number of things in common.

We're both Latina, we're both the oldest child, and we're both very determined people. Like me, she cares about her family, especially about her brothers. And she's a reader! Being an avid reader myself, I'm impressed that she's well-read and interested in all kinds of books. So why are her grades barely passable? Maybe a mentor with some tutoring background can help her catch up.

Now it seems that once she starts talking, wild horses can't stop her. I'm not sure if she's always this talkative once comfortable, but I listen to it all.

She's actually quite fascinating and the conversation extends all the way back home. We're almost there when I again broach the subject of a mentor.

"Wasn't that lasagna great? I go to this restaurant specifically for their lasagna but the garlic bread is pretty good too."

"Yeah, it was awesome!" She nods enthusiastically.

"The best thing is that I can trust the people there to always have great service and lasagna. Trust is important in any transaction or relationship. Today, you had a chance to know me a little better, so I am hoping that you can trust me to find you a great mentor. I promise that she'll be someone you can trust and who will help you finish high school, as well as plan for your future. In fact, I already have a woman in mind. But I'll leave it to you to decide if it's a good match. Will you give the program a try?"

"Yeah, I guess so."

"I'm asking you to meet me halfway. I get you an awesome mentor, and you agree to meet with her on a weekly basis so that she can get to know you and help you. Agreed?"

"Yeah, okay, I can do that"

"You're going to need to apply for the program. I'll give you a blank application when we get to your house. By the way, I am so glad I brought you today. You were a big help and a great lunch companion!"

"That's okay." She suddenly looks away. "Can I turn on your radio the rest of the way home?"

I'm glad she has asked politely to listen to the radio, but suspect that she's a bit embarrassed by the compliment.

As we park in front of her home, I reach into my bag for a blank application, reminding her, "Here's the paperwork. Please get it in as soon as possible… this week, alright?"

"Okay." She takes the paper and starts to exit the car.

"I promise you that you're going to get a great mentor, so expect to hear from me soon."

She mumbles, "Thanks," and, as if trying out my name to see if it's okay to say, adds, "Angie, thanks for lunch and everything."

I want to say something better than the standard *you're welcome* so I blurt out, "In the meantime, feel free to stop by my office if you ever want to talk."

I don't know what possesses me to say that, but I'm sure she'll forget it by day's end. She's a court kid, after all, and is used to court personnel trying to make kids comfortable with the various programs. It's not until I deposit her at her doorstep that I realize we never talked about the seminar. But it's okay; there will be time for the mentor to ask her.

The important thing is that I have gotten her off her island, this island she uses to protect herself from whatever else is going on in her world. I know it might just be temporary, but I also know that, like my other "court kids," once matched with her own special mentor, she might be ready to consider the world of opportunity ahead.

ANGIE CARRERA has been writing since the age of eight, focusing mostly on poetry and short stories. Retired from local government, she volunteers for her church community and teaches classes to bilinguals seeking to become professional or community interpreters. She loves sharing her home with her lively mother, hanging out with friends, and watching her five handsome grandnephews and two beautiful granddaughters grow. She credits the extraordinary storytellers at Writers of Chantilly with all they have taught her about the fine art of writing. Encouraged by her fellow writers and cheered on by her sweetheart, she is currently working on her first fiction novel for young adults.

LOVE'S CRIMSON CARESS
ANGELA D. GLASCOCK

I plucked the sand dollar, purple and covered in fine bristles, from the golden sand. Lifting it to my face, I smiled for a moment before tossing it beyond the waves, where it would have a better chance for survival.

The storm last night had washed all kinds of flotsam onto my beach, each, I suspected, with its own story. I'd already found a leather deck shoe, a cooler, and frosted turquoise sea glass A man's voice jerked me from my beachcombing. .

For most people, to hear voices while walking on a beach is not uncommon. For me, it's rare.

I turned, for the voice came from behind. There was a man, shouting and waving his hands over his head like he was flagging down an airplane.

I don't like people. I find them exhausting. It's a struggle for me to be just a fraction less awkward than I am. I'm never successful and end up drawing everyone around me into my discomfort. For this and other reasons, I worked very hard to isolate myself.

Hence, my own private, *secluded* island.

I responded to him with a shooing gesture. He gave me a pageant wave, just like Miss America. If only people still communicated with flags – I could fly one that indicated this island was plague-ridden.

The man came closer, walking on my sand like it was a

public beach. I could hear his voice, but couldn't understand what he said because of the wind and distance.

This would be a nice occasion to have a little pistol, one of those derringers characters in novels pull from some risqué hiding place – a boot, a garter, a brassiere. I've always wanted to work that into my fiction.

Me, I could store one in my fanny pack with the seashells and sea glass.

You would be surprised at how many islands aren't truly secluded. I know this because when I was shopping for islands, I noticed the mainland was visible from many of them. That was too close to civilization for me. After nearly a year of searching, I found this small gem in the South Pacific.

How was I, a middle-aged, overweight, widowed romance novelist able to afford such extravagance? People probably think my husband left a fortune when he died. Alas, people would be wrong. He left nothing but a broken heart.

Along with money saved from book sales and cash from a generous great-grandfather's estate, I was able to acquire Island Es-ay, or SA, as in *Stay Away*. Its previous name was Blue Duck Island, but I changed it to something more informative. Besides, I've never seen any ducks here, blue or otherwise.

I prided myself on being self-sufficient. If the world ended, I could survive for a year before I'd get uncomfortable. There were only two required occasions for me to have contact with humanity: when I needed to restock, which I did quarterly because it reduced the amount of cargo for each trip, and when I needed to mail a manuscript and floppy discs containing said manuscript to my publisher.

This is why it was a shock to hear a human voice other than my own while beachcombing.

"Excuse me, miss?"

I snorted. My days of being a "miss" were but a far and foggy memory. He'd obviously been in the sun too long.

"Miss." He pulled the ball cap off his head. "I was wondering if you could help me."

"Yes. I can help you by informing you that you're trespassing on private property."

He stood there, kneading his cap with his hands and squinting in the sunlight. "I, um, I was looking for someone."

"Well, you're not going to find them here."

His hands dropped to his sides and he slumped; a kite that lost its wind. "So this isn't Bernadette Pearlson's place?"

"Who wants to know?"

"Me—I'm Keith Rose."

"'Keith Rose?'" What kind of name is Keith Rose? Sounded like a crappy pop singer's name.

I looked him up and down. He wore a Hawaiian shirt and board shorts that were too big. His hair was long, blond, and wavy. His skin was tan, his nose burnt and peeling. He looked like he was maybe twenty, but when he squinted in the sun, I could see lines that belonged on an older face.

"It's just that Ms. Pearlson is my most favorite author." He nodded with a close-lipped grin. "She's radical. Cutting edge. You know…." He trailed off as he glanced around.

"What do you have in your hand there, Mr. Rose?"

"Please, call me Keith." He raised his hand, smiling with

his lips pressed together. "It's one of Ms. Pearlson's books."

A hot spark zapped through my bitter soul. I caught a glimpse of the photo I'd chosen for the back cover; it wasn't me. My publisher and I decided it was best if we used a younger picture. Of someone else. I closed my eyes and took a deep breath.

"Isn't this Ms. Pearlson's property?" He scratched his head with the corner of the book.

"Maybe. Doesn't matter. You're trespassing."

"Oh." He stepped back. "I was in the neighborhood—"

"—'The neighborhood'?"

"Yes. I'm moving a boat for a…friend. I remembered an article in *Life* about Ms. Pearlson and her island. And when I was charting my route I thought, 'Rad! I'll be near her island. Maybe I can get an autograph!'"

The paperback he clutched caught my attention: *Love's Crimson Caress. A new series by beloved romance writer Bernadette Pearlson!*

The new series was a huge flop. Teenage vampires. What was I thinking? Kids today were into *Knight Rider* and *Music Television*. They were more interested in Atari and Sony Walkmans and Boomboxes and breakdancing than reading.

"Excuse me?" I said. Rose was still talking, but I'd gotten lost in my thoughts again.

"I said she's my favorite author. Her other series is pretty awesome, but this new one is like, primo." He paused, studying the area. "The pictures in *Life,* of the island, the dock. This looks just like them. And I charted it., but…am I on the wrong island?"

I softened. Primo. I'd always considered myself an excellent judge of character, and this guy seemed harmless. I held out my hand for the book. "Okay. I'll autograph it for you."

He said nothing but stood there looking confused.

"I'm Bernadette Pearlson. This is Island Estefay."

His eyes bounced from the back cover to me and back again.

"It's a stock photo," I said.

A smile lit up his face and he handed me the book.

I raised my eyebrows as I held out my hand. "Pen?"

He checked his pockets, the grin sliding from his face as he turned in place, scanning the sand.

"No pen?"

"I had a pen. I had it with me. It's this gold pen from…I can't believe this."

I smiled. "I have plenty of pens in the cottage. Then you can be on your way." I turned, gesturing him to follow. "Since you're pretty much the only fan of the *Crimson* series, I'll make an exception. My cottage is back this way."

Inside the cottage, I offered Keith a drink.

"Wow. I can't believe I'm with Bernadette Pearlson," he said.

Heat tickled my cheeks. Was I *blushing?*

"I read your other series, but this new one—the *Crimson* series?—it's like nothing else I've read."

I set a glass of water on the table in front of him. "You're different than my usual fan base."

Now it was Keith who blushed. "I know. But is so…relatable."

I cocked my head. *Relatable?* Okay.

I slid into the cane chair as I pulled the worn book to me, opened it to the title page, wrote a short note, then signed my name. I slid the book back to him.

We were quiet for an uncomfortable moment.

"Well. Keith, as interesting as this has been, I have a deadline. So. It was nice to meet you." I went to the door but he didn't follow. "Mr. Rose? Keith? I really need to get back to work."

He'd paused in front of one of my many bookshelves, opened the glass door protecting its contents, and removed a book. "Is this a first edition Ernest Hemingway?"

I strode to him and plucked *The Sun Also Rises* from his hands. "Please. Don't touch. It's rare."

"I remember when it was first published."

"What?" I scowled. "That's not possible. It was published before even I was born." I returned the book to the shelf and closed the door. "It's time for you to go."

He turned to me and offered a smile so toothy, it was more like baring his teeth at me. I could see why he'd kept his lips together when he'd smiled before. His teeth were broken, jagged, and a deep red—*crimson*—stained most of them.

His tone and body language had completely changed. I stepped back.

He pulled the door open again and trailed a finger down an ancient copy of *Sense and Sensibility*. "Jane Austen. A lovely woman. Died too soon. Still had so much left to tell, to write."

His eyes darted from one titled to another.

He clapped his hands together, which made me jump. "Mary Shelley's *The Last Man!* One of my favorites, even then, when everyone else dismissed it. Devoted to her husband, was Mary. And a widow, like you, Ms. Pearlson." He turned to me. "Tell me, how do you get supplies? It's a long way from the mainland. What if there was an emergency?"

I turned and went straight for the fireplace, where I yanked a poker from its stand. "Get out of my house."

"I was just asking. Dear me. You act like I'm some kind of…monster." He crossed the room and strode out the door, not bothering to shut it behind him.

I slammed the door and locked it. Still carrying the poker, I climbed the stairs as fast as my out-of-shape body would allow, stepping out onto the upper deck then climbing more stairs to the crow's nest. I laid the poker down on a bench, then pulled binoculars out from beneath another.

I scanned the beach and dock, searching for Keith Rose, but I couldn't locate him. His boat was still there.

I ran back downstairs, sweat beading on my forehead and dampening my shirt. I checked each door and window to be sure they were locked before I picked up the phone.

No dial tone.

I took a deep breath as I replaced the receiver in the cradle. Sometimes the phone went out, especially after a storm.

I poured myself a glass of scotch to calm my nerves. I sipped it, thinking.

Tomorrow morning I'd take my boat to the mainland. Maybe stay in a hotel for a few days, maybe reconsider my security, or lack thereof, maybe get a couple of Dobermans, like in *Magnum, PI.*

And a gun.

I returned to the kitchen to refresh my scotch. When I saw the book that lay on the table, and what was next to it, the glass slipped from my grasp, shattering on the tile floor. It was the same worn copy of *Love's Crimson Caress* I'd signed for Keith earlier; next to it was a rose so dark red it was almost black.

Crimson.

ANGELA D. GLASCOCK has been a writer from the time she was able to hold a writing utensil. However, it took her until college to realize that writing was her calling. She has a blog called "Biggest, Brightest Star in the Sky: Mostly True Tales." She is an editorial writer for The Greenbriar Flyer and is working on two non-fiction books and the second part of her self-published book, Locksmith at the End of the World: A Dead Silence Novella, *which is available at Amazon.com and CreateSpace.com. She also handcrafts award-winning jewelry.*

PAT'S PICKS
PATRICIA BOSWELL KALLMAN

Back when I was a teenager, a long time ago when we didn't have Facebook or Twitter to help us voice our opinions, Slam Books were all the rage. You usually made your own Slam Book out of half sheets of paper attached together with a decorative cover, and then, surreptitiously passed it around to your classmates. The first page had a list of numbers down the side. Participants picked a number and put their name next to it. Each page of the book had a question at the top. The question might be a simple "What is your favorite color?" or a more complicated "You're going to be on a deserted island for the rest of your life. What three books would you choose to take with you?" Your friends would write their answer to the question, underline it and put their number from the front page under the line. Supposedly this gave everyone anonymity, but of course we all memorized our potential boyfriend's or girlfriend's number from the first page and paid close attention to their answers throughout.

The deserted island question cropped up a lot, with some variations. After a bit, the question was refined to: "You're going to be on a deserted island for the rest of your life. What three books would you choose to take with you besides The Bible, *The Complete Works of Shakespeare,* and a first aid/survival book?" At that point, the answers started to get more interesting and revealing.

Being an avid reader all my life, I'm sure I had plenty of fodder for the answer to this question, but I can't help thinking about what my choices might be today as a seventy-year-old. It's a tough one, but it could be a bit easier now that I only have thirty years or so to fill!

Okay, I've got the three mentioned above, although I am going to jettison The Bible and the first aid/survival book in favor of a couple others. I'd rather go out with a good read in my hand than be trying to fix something impossible to fix because I'm on a deserted island.

Anyway, it's still miserably hard to pick individual books. Since it is *my* essay, I'm thinking of changing it to "the bodies of work" by three different authors, or six authors, if I get three freebies to start with. I still go back and forth endlessly trying to zero in on my choices. I'd have to get past the inclination to go for the world's greatest literature. I'd think my answer would reflect books that would be a joy or comfort to me in a solitary existence.

Even though I can think of at least a hundred worthy authors who have turned out tons of lovely tomes, I guess I want my authors routinely to take me somewhat beyond the "good read" category, whose writing would give me an insight or two into other eras and human character, achievement and foibles. I guess, since I'm all alone, I don't have to read about politics and hateful societal failings. I think I'd actually ditch non-fiction completely. I'm not so much into science fiction and fantasy, although even there I have some favorites. I would probably want to lean toward optimistic themes. I do love a good human predicament though.

My mind races through my childhood book friends. So many that I loved. I think through my twenties and thirties, full of thought-provoking exploration, enlightenment and cutting edges. I can't even begin to pare down the poets. Then there are my mature choices of mystery and fun that help me switch gears at bedtime and drift into sleep for a while. I start to pick my top contenders, but there are too many competitors to list. I'd gladly discuss these with you sometime, if you want. I'm certain I would spend many happy hours on my island just remembering all my favorites.

I need authors who write beautifully. I must have consummate storytellers. I crave the ones who craft humor or wonder with every word they write. I want to be encouraged by those who write everything well. I require that they'll help me escape my island, and give me courage to carry on when I am washed back ashore.

All right, so here they are: Shakespeare, Jane Austin and Mark Twain. These were the no-brainers for me, the must-haves. Add to that Mary Stewart, Ursula K. Le Guin and Paul Gallico. Yes, I know, I said I didn't much care for fantasy, but Ursula is in a class by herself. Yes, I do know there are so many deserving others, but my island, my list.

Since I'm bending the rules quite a bit already, I think I'd also like to hit that beach with a lifetime supply of paper and pencils. I'm sure my "library" would inspire me to create many drafts of my own magnum opus.

When my Slam Book comes around to you, it will contain the question above. What are your picks for your deserted island?

1._____
2._____
3._____

Your Number Here

STEADER
NICHOLAS BRUNER

1

"I would give my left ovary for a glass of pinot grigio," Medea said to the figure on the screen of her tablet. "I mean it, Treva. I could kill a man for a bottle of wine right now."

Treva laughed. "Don't go stir crazy on us now! We'll see you in two days. And we're stocked—all the wine you want to trade for."

"Oh, one more thing," Medea said. "I haven't been getting a full charge in my powerwall. I need to get somebody to look at it."

"Uh oh," Treva said. "Definitely don't want anything messing with your power. Any idea what the problem is?"

"I checked but didn't see anything obvious." Medea idly ran her thumb along a patch of sea salt flaked on the table. "Could be the inverter, maybe."

"Ask Henry to take a look at it," Treva said. "He takes care of all our equipment like that here."

"Great. Two days then. Looking forward to it."

"Us too, honey. It's been too long."

Medea closed the cover on the tablet and tossed it into the seat next to her. Out the window, the sun approached its highest point and curly white cirrus clouds wisped to the horizon. Medea smiled and rose, exiting the center living module and striding along the deck. Her steadcraft was a perfect circle, two-hundred-forty feet across, and fully self-sustaining. Rows of corn bobbed gently in the constant sea breeze, and the vines of heirloom tomato plants hung heavy-laden from their metal cages.

She and Jason had thought about making their own wine, but the trellises required for the grapes would have been too tall—would have interfered with the gliding of the solar panels and the drip irrigation. Same with the apples and peaches she longed for. Trees would grow way too high, plus the roots would spread underneath the deck. It was amazing how much growth could be packed on such a small surface, but only with careful consideration of the space required for each addition. Well, maybe they'd have some fruit at Puerto Libre to trade for.

She stopped at the raised lip at the edge of the deck and leaned against the railing, staring out at the sea. Hecate appeared from somewhere, rubbed against Medea's legs, meowed, and leapt up to the top so she could better scratch his head. It never ceased to terrify her when he strolled along the rail, where one false step could plunge him into the brine, but he did not notice the danger. She petted him and slipped an arm under his body, lifting him away from the edge.

"Down you go! No need to feed the sharks today."

Nearly midday, time to adjust the solar panels. She climbed up and shifted them along the tracks on their framework, maneuvering them over the potatoes and carrots, where they would provide needed shade for these cool weather plants. She pressed a switch and tilted the panels to maximize their sun exposure. With the powerwall leaky, she wanted to soak up all the power she could get.

Morning chores done, and a half hour to lunch. Just enough time to catch some rays.

One thing you couldn't beat was the tanning.

Lying out on the sundeck above the living module, the hot sun spreading across her body like melting butter, temperature balanced by the perpetual breeze of the open ocean. She reveled in the solitude of being the only living soul for a hundred miles or more.

Not that she didn't get lonely sometimes. It hadn't always been that way. Before, Jason had been there, and the two of them had been enough. Working on the steadcraft in the morning—he could've fixed the powerwall in an hour, while she tended to the vegetables and herbs. Scrabble after dinner. Splitting a bottle of wine. Making love at night and—why not?—again the next morning.

She traced a finger around her earlobe, across her cheek, as he used to do with his flicking tongue. Lightly along her neck, her sternum, around the outer edge of her breast, the areola, down her stomach, across the shallow indention of the femoral triangle, her breathing quickening and excitement spreading from her inner thighs. Her foot pointed and she raised a knee slightly to allow the tips of her fingers—

She froze.

Medea felt something she had not felt in a long time. She almost laughed out loud to think it, it was so impossible. Here, in the one place it could not possibly happen.

She felt that someone was watching her.

Silly.

Still, the spooky sensation ended her tanning session. She rose and put a towel around her, shaking her head at herself. Oh, well. She needed to cut some mint from the garden for her lunch salad anyway. Maybe pluck some motherwort leaves to crush into a calming herbal tea.

Medea sipped her tea. A bit bitter for her taste, but Treva would have some lemons. She already felt the calm spread through her body, numbing the bizarreness of the tanning incident. She knew the source of that invasive feeling, of course. Obvious, once she reflected on it.

That fishing vessel she'd met four days ago. Hailed her on the radio, asked if she wanted to trade. Not so unusual to see another vessel on occasion, a little less so to interact, but not unheard of. A Korean-flagged boat with a mixed crew.

Steaders were known for providing substances illicit in much the rest of the world. Medea had made it plain she didn't have any of that. The smiling, bronze-faced Korean man, the captain, explained in surprisingly good English: "We have plenty tuna, no vegetables. Out here two more weeks. What you give for tuna?"

Hadn't seemed like a bad deal at the time. Get rid of her excess of cucumbers and squash. Throw in some eggs. Stock up her deep freezer with fish. Favorable terms of trade, too.

The Korean captain had showed concern that she was out on the high seas by herself. "You all alone out here?"

He'd given her an avuncular smile and his words had a friendly tone, but they reminded her of things past. She'd glanced around, suddenly aware she was the only woman, with a crew of perhaps a dozen men on the other side. She squashed a tendril of irrational fear and smiled back. "I like it that way."

He'd squinted at her steadcraft and back at her. "You handle that big thing by yourself?" She'd assured him she had been handling it by herself for a long time now.

Not much about the crew stuck her now, except for one man. Stayed off to the side, by himself. And no wonder, with burns covering much of his face. She hadn't so much seen him as *not* seen him, intentionally averting her eyes. But she had found her line of sight drifting towards him once or twice, his fleece stocking cap worn even in the tropical air, his fascinatingly marred features sagging molten folds across his cheeks as if he'd only just stepped out of the flames and his skin were still soft.

He'd sensed her interest and stared back. Hardness behind those eyes. An onion peeler of a gaze. Like he'd stripped her down of her clothes and her skin too.

She'd thought about him later, reviewed that wilting face in her mind: cheese in the toaster oven, a watch in a Dali painting. What kind of place could a man like that have in society? A tuna boat in the middle of the Pacific, that was the place.

She snapped her fingers. *Right, the tuna.* If she wanted a tuna steak for dinner, she'd better set it out to thaw. Actually, it was probably too late for today. She'd have to stick it in the fridge so it'd be ready tomorrow.

They had Jason by the arms, two of them. It was surprising how small they were, not big men at all. Short and acne-scarred and big-eared, grinning at their prize. A third one sauntered up and walloped Jason in his belly. A thump and an audible groan. All Medea could do was stare.

He glanced up at her, silently mouthing the words: "Go! Godammit, go!" And then a fourth one, the leader, had pulled out a butterfly knife and she cringed to see what happened next. The blood flowed from Jason's side, but she felt the heat against her chest, as if that blade had slid right between her own ribs.

Medea sat straight up in her bed, her hair a mess of sweat. Hecate leaped to the floor, miffed at the disturbance. She patted the sheets were he'd lain, the warm spot where he'd nestled against her side. Odd for him to sleep right next to her instead of his preferred spot at her feet. Still, that explained the one part of her nightmare, at least.

What's gotten into me?

And then it struck her. It was the first of August. The anniversary was only one day away. She'd pushed it out of her head, but she must have known subconsciously. She checked her watch: 5:00 AM. Well, she might as well get up and do the chores.

First thing was the chickens. Medea got a bowl of feed and spread it around the chicken coop, drawing the half dozen hens from wherever they unhurriedly pecked for worms and insects.

"Good morning, ladies. What do you have for me today?" She checked the coop and found three eggs. Fine – two for breakfast and one to refrigerate. Worrisome though. This was the third day in a row with low production. Normally she got five or six. "Lucy? Brigitte? Aren't you ladies feeling well?

Not a lot of seasteaders kept chickens—too messy. But

Medea found they kept her company, and eggs provided a nice addition to fish. Their droppings were high in nitrogen, great for the tomato plants. Plus, a couple dozen fresh eggs were always a nice bonus to throw in if a bartering partner was balking at an exchange.

She stopped and plucked a couple ripe tomatoes to add to her omelette. One had a rotten hole in it. Hopefully they weren't infested. Fruitworms could spread to the corn and the okra. On a steadcraft, that would really play havoc with carefully planned menus and trade goods. She'd have to check later for eggs on the leaves.

She opened the refrigerator, searching for the peanut butter. Not in its usual place. *Did I finish the jar already?* Something else to trade with Treva for. She made a mental note to add it to her list.

A crash from outside, a flurry of squawks and clucks and feathers rustling. Medea dashed towards the coop, nearly tripping over Hecate sprinting in the opposite direction with tail outstretched. A roosting bar had fallen against the mesh wire floor. An ungodly racket, but not a huge problem. She could fix it later.

That damn cat. But it was strange. Hecate was well-fed, and he'd never been too concerned with the chickens before. *Good God, I'd better eat my breakfast before something else breaks.*

The ocean drank the red setting sun, sending bloody streaks across the waves from horizon to horizon. In the north, a hint of black mounted, lit from time to time by tendrils of lightning. Medea checked the weather report again. The storm had come up from out of nowhere, but that could happen out here on a late summer afternoon in the warm waters of the mid-Pacific. If she wanted to make civilization by the morning, she'd have to power through it. Well, a little rain never hurt anyone.

In the kitchen she sliced lettuce, onions, cilantro, and tomatoes. Lemons would have been the perfect final touch, but still, she had enough for a salad with her fish. She expertly cut the tomatoes into quarters. One tomato was bad; black and mushy on one side. *Fruit worms.*

"That's it!" She marched out to the tomato plants. She had to find the eggs before this became a real problem. Only all the plants looked fine. Healthy, reddening tomatoes. Maybe in the morning she'd check again. She saw something on the ground out of the corner of her eye and leaned over. A brown seed.

She picked it up. Teardrop-shaped. An apple seed. But she didn't have any apples. Slowly, an idea seeped into her consciousness.

The tanning incident hadn't been just a feeling.

She was truly not alone.

Medea stood frozen for long moments, not daring to turn her head. But she did, finally. Nobody was there. She exhaled, realizing only then she'd been holding her breath.

She was being ridiculous. Nobody was on board. Where would they even hide? And an apple seed? Could've come from anywhere. One of the sailors had gobbed it out when they'd brought the fish over and it'd landed on her deck. Or it was from long ago.

But...still. It could be. A stranger, unwelcome. On her floating island. It seemed almost impossible, but it wasn't, really. It was a bit smaller than average as steaders went, but there were numerous crannies, gaps behind equipment, even the honeycombed foam lining the hull.

She sniffed the air. Something was burning. The tuna steak. She dashed back to the galley.

Medea carved around the charred portion of the tuna. There was quite a bit salvageable, but she still wasn't hungry for it. She forced herself to eat, knowing she would need the energy this night. At the very least, she had to search every inch of the place. She picked up the dishes and brought them to the sink, washed them deliberately while she thought.

Let's say there is an intruder. Think it out. Would she confront him head-on? She would have to, at some point. Obviously, if he was there, he'd come on board from the fishing boat. Now he was hidden somewhere on the steadcraft, had been for days, watching her, eating her produce, staring at her lustfully while she tanned or slept.

Maybe she should have kept Jason's gun. The only thing they'd ever really argued about, and she'd traded it away months before. But she decided she was better off without it—after all, the intruder could have used it on her any time since he'd boarded.

And that was another matter. He'd had four days. Why hadn't he attacked her yet? Surely he wasn't just a stowaway. What was he waiting for?

She shook her head. *So juvenile, Medea.* She'd give the steadcraft a good once-over for her peace of mind, and go to bed.

And then the lights went out.

2

Medea stood corpse-still, hands still immersed in soapy water. *Stay calm. It's a problem with the powerwall, that's all.* She'd been having issues with it. Something had gone wrong, a loose connection, a frayed wire.

But she knew that wasn't right. It was on purpose. *Think, Medea, think. Say there is an intruder on the ship. Why hasn't he done anything? And why the power drain? There has to be a reason.* A wine cork bobbed in the dishwater, spinning around in the bubbles. Kind of like a mini-steadcraft. Maybe there was a little miniature Medea on the top of that cork, waiting for some bad guy cork to come along. Medea gasped. *That's it!*

She dried her hands, grabbed a pair of binoculars. As she climbed the metal ladder to the tanning deck, a few drops of rain splashed on her skin, the leading edge of the storm. Wind had picked up, too.

She put the binoculars to her eyes and scanned the ocean. There, due east, on the very edge of the horizon. A dingy catamaran. Fast though, the kind preferred by pirates. Appear out of nowhere, attack a cargo ship or a steadcraft, gone before help can arrive. That's what the intruder had been waiting on. He'd been signaling. Probably explained the powerwall drain too, powering some beacon or emitter. And now, once they'd established visual contact, cut the power.

How long did she have? From this vantage point, the distance to the horizon was eight miles. A catamaran like that should cover twice that distance in an hour, but the waves were choppy. Might be more like forty-five minutes. No time to waste, in any case.

Back in the dark living module, she didn't need light; she knew this place well. In the kitchen, she led her fingers across the countertop to the wooden knife block and selected the fish scaling knife with its comfortable grip and thick blade, whistle-sharp on its curved side and serrated on the other. *Just in case.*

Outside again, rain falling steadily now, fat drops collecting in her hair and sliding cold down her back. Down the spiral staircase into the powerwall room, the rubbery surface of the non-slip stairs compressing under her bare feet and one sweaty hand gripping the knife.

Red and green glowing and blinking dots came into view, and she stopped on the bottom stair to calm her breath. The blinking lights were a good sign.

It was completely quiet in the narrow room, without the usual low hum from the equipment. Still, from what she could tell, the powerwall had simply been shut down rather than damaged in some way. All she had to do was press the main power switch and it should start up on its own. Other electronics on the boat might require restarting too, but she could figure that out later.

She ran her hands along the surface, searching for the indentation of the power switch. A creak from behind her. She stopped, slowly swiveled her head.

In the back corner a figure crouched, about five feet away, dark, hooded. He'd certainly noticed her. Neither moved for a long minute. A low rumble of thunder resonated outside, vibrating the boat to its core.

It was amazing how calm she felt, now that it was true.

The figure leaped at her and she jabbed upwards with

her knife hand, but the knife glided over leather and into free air and the figure was quick, catching her around the waist and knocking her to the floor. Her head and shoulder thudded painfully against the bricked batteries of the powerwall. He was on top of her and sour sweat and body odor filled her nostrils. The arms constricted around her, shoving her along the bumpy floor, roughly groping her back, her arms, her breasts, finding her throat and squeezing. Each individual finger dug in until she could feel tendons in her neck split.

No air and no thoughts, only pure panic. But somehow in her state she had held onto the knife and she jammed it into his side, drove it until the point punctured leather. Deeper then, into pulp and bouncing against bone. The figure reared back and spat curses in a foreign tongue. He pushed himself up and staggered up the stairs. She managed one look at his face as he fled in the dim light.

The right side was covered in burn scarring.

Medea gulped air for several breaths without sitting up. She put a hand to her face, to her neck. Tender, but nothing broken. Probably lots and lots of bruising later.

Her eyes blinked closed and she faded. For a moment, she screwed up her resolve and opened them, trying to will herself from passing out. Her eyes fluttered closed again and things went black.

That night again. She had heeded Jason's command, fled while she could, but to where? Their steadcraft was occupied so the only place she could go was the pirates' boat, sneaking up the gangplank, not that stealth was necessary as drunk as they all were. Nasty old catamaran greasy with diesel fumes. But they used kerosene for their personal use—cooking, most likely. She'd spread the contents of that fifty-gallon drum all across the deck, the personal quarters, the control room, against a backdrop of the men's inebriated laughter and her husband's screams and begging for his life in the black air.

She'd been patient, waiting for the pirates to return, sloshed and jolly with their evil, carrying away what they wanted as booty—bottles of wine, her jewelry, sonar, satellite radio equipment—and she'd slipped quietly overboard and back to her own vessel, but not before lighting a match.

It'd been positively beautiful as she'd engaged the engines and, with a jerk, pulled away from the orange-blue funeral pyre. She'd held Jason's lifeless body in her arms, its face so swollen and blued with bruising she couldn't recognize him. But the screams of burning men provided a measure of satisfaction, and she had gorged herself on them. Sound carries a long way on open water.

Medea came to and her eyes snapped open. Still slumped in the dim glow of the powerwall. Tired. Achy. She wanted to go back to sleep, but knew she couldn't. Had to find the intruder. But she suspected he was in worse shape than her, as that wound of his continued to bleed.

She grabbed the knife and forced herself to her feet, stumbled to the far end of the powerwall, initiated power up. It responded without any problems, though it would take several minutes for everything to come back online, at least what didn't need to be restarted manually. She found the magnetic penknife attached to the powerwall for occasions just such as this and slipped it in her pocket.

Medea tried to stand straight. Her knees staggered. She nearly fell, only barely catching the handrail of the stairs as a swirl of dizziness overtook her. Carefully she made her way up the stairs to the deck. Rain spit in the open door at the top and she closed it behind her. She was soaked almost as soon as she stepped out. Water spouted out of the sky, and it was nearly pitch black.

She had to get to the living module, boot up the guidance and steering computer. She stumbled around, nausea rumbling in her gut as she tried to stay on the paths, slipping repeatedly to the ground. It was taking much longer than it should—in her disorientation and the dark, she'd somehow lost her way. A flash of lightning gave a glimpse of the whirling sea, and she realized the dizziness was not her—it was the steadcraft. Of course, without power, there was no rudder control. They were spinning freely across the ocean.

Another lurch knocked her down again, where she came face to a face with a chicken sitting and miserably dripping right in the middle of the path.

"Oh, Lucy," Medea said. "What are doing out in this weather?" But her words were lost in the wind. She picked the soaking bird up, tucked it under her arm, baby steps to the henhouse. Another round of lightning and she saw the door had blown off the coop. And in the herb garden, lit briefly like a stadium, half the plants lay trampled to the dirt by bootprints.

Medea gritted her teeth. *That asshole.* At least she knew which direction he'd gone.

She stuck her head inside the coop. The hens were lined up along the top perch, nervously clucking. She gently placed Lucy among her sisters. Odd. Lucy was one of the more sensible ones. Maybe she'd simply been caught by a gust of wind when the door blew off. Anyway, the henhouse was bolted to the deck, so they should all be safe enough. As safe as anything on a night like this. Medea was almost tempted to curl up in the relative dryness of the henhouse herself.

She ducked out and a hand grabbed her hair and pulled her down, forcing her face into cold mud. She slashed out ineffectually with the knife, but another hand had her now by her upper arm, yanked her back to her feet, and she got her first good look at the man: no taller than she, his black hair slicked back in the wetness, water running diagonally along the burn grooves on his cheek.

"Three years," he hissed in her ear, heavy accent pronouncing the three as 'tree.' "Three years I search for you. Three years I wait. My companions, dead. All dead. And me, six months in burn unit. After, my face. Hideous. But tonight, you know pain like me."

Pain? This was the man who'd crushed her motherwort. This was the man who'd helped kill her husband. And this was the man who had—

A squall cut her thought short, the boat listed wildly, and they tumbled together across the deck, through a patch of corn. Medea's stomach twisted as much from nausea as from seeing her hard-worked crops battered and flattened.

He lost his grip on her, but they were still entangled. She got to her feet first while he was on his knees. She swung at his face but he blocked her knife hand. More lightning illuminated the scene, and she saw something he didn't. He rose, she ducked, and a free swinging steel bar hit him in the back of the head and knocked him to the ground. Part of the irrigation and solar panel framework. Another damn thing that would have to be fixed in the morning, but she could hardly feel more grateful for it now.

But the man was not out yet. He crawled across the deck. She ran after and kicked at him; he grabbed her foot and she tripped. Another lurch, another sheet of rain, and she lost track of him. No—there he was, he'd somehow found a hatch and heaved it open, disappearing inside. A little used compartment that led to the keel, used only for occasional repairs.

Aching, knife in one hand and penlight between teeth, Medea crawled through the foam lining honeycombed around the hull of the steadcraft. She had followed the intermittent drips of water and blood down here, to the true bowels of the ship. The passages provided room enough for movement on hands and knees and no more.

She halted to catch her breath and listen. Yes, up ahead, somewhere in the maze, the squeak of pressure against polyurethane. She popped the penknife back in her mouth and set off. She wasn't sure if she was on the hunt or prey heading straight into the trap, but she was eager to end this chase.

Left, left, straight for a while. She came to a pile of trash—eggshells (had he eaten them raw?), chocolate bar wrappers, an empty jar of peanut butter (aha!). And a plastic case, about two feet square. She opened it. It housed a mechanical device, face covered with knobs and switches, a spool of wire on the top. *The transmitter.* He must have used the wire to plug into the powerwall at night. *How many hours did he sit up on the deck with that while I was sleeping?*

She pushed all the junk aside and crawled onwards, around a vertical loop that flipped her on her back, requiring her to roll over, penlight beam flitting crazily across the white walls. A moist smear of blood across the white surface where he must have passed only moments before. She redoubled her pace now, right, left, and around the next corner she could hear his breathing, even heavier than hers, ragged and uneven. He must know she was there. Her knuckles showed white where she gripped the knife.

Moments. Minutes. The only sounds their panting, rhythmic, inhalations and exhalations phasing into and out of synchronization. It was impossible to tell how long. She flipped the light off. All is equal in the dark, right? She lunged around the corner.

Stabbing, knife hitting a boot and glancing off. She forced it again farther up, skidding off the foam wall, his rough hand sliding across her face until it slipped into her hair and pulled her on top of him, their breathing in synch again, faces inches apart. His hot breath was in her ear, his grotesque face touching her cheek, and her instrument finally finding purchase; a wet place she twisted with sickening glee. This close, that sour sweat smell again, it felt almost…intimate.

That night, three years ago, it flowed back to her. The pirate ship, somebody's bed chamber. He and the other pirates having their way with her, but he chiefly, his face not mortified then, but rough with whiskers, handsome maybe under different circumstances. Jason back on the steadcraft, tied up, helpless, she hoped she might buy his life with a good performance, so she acted like she loved it. Screaming with theatre, with simulated ecstasy, but hating every second and loathing them all, her revulsion all the greater because of her act. She had made her body respond, arched her back, meeting each thrust for every man, thinking that would satisfy them. And when it didn't, when they'd dragged her wrung out back to her own steadcraft and made her watch their fun with her husband, deep inside her a craving had grown for vengeance.

Her revenge that night, the consuming fire, had been enough for what they'd done to Jason, but not for what they'd done to her. And now here she had her chance to truly return the favor, to penetrate this man, to give to him what he had given to her. She ground the knife deeper. Did he appreciate it? Yes, he did, moaning as she rammed the knife as far as it would go and blood-streaked spittle bubbled out his lips. He jolted and then his body relaxed under her.

The storm must have separated the steadcraft from the pirate ship. *Hopefully the bastards sank to the bottom of the ocean,* Medea thought as she steered the ship in the early morning sun. Rain had scrubbed the steadcraft, and the world, clean. Bushes laden with berries glistened, water collecting beneath them in fat drops and falling to the deck with little brilliant splashes. Newly brave chickens ventured forth for their morning feed. Hecate rubbed against her legs. And in the far distance, something glinted white.

It gradually came into view. Puerto Libre. An island, a whole community, of steaders, boats abutting or connected with planks or even elaborate pedestrian bridges, some growing crops, some with workshops or junkyards or trading posts or mini-foundries.

Medea coolly glided around the right side of the mass of steadcraft, smiling when the blue-and-white checkerboard pattern of her destination came into view. Treva's place—and there she was, brown hair in ringlets, arms folded and supporting her weight at the viewing deck. She spied Medea and gathered up her peasant skirt, running down to her main level in bare feet. Medea expertly pulled her magnetic latching gate to where it met Treva's and cut the propulsion.

Treva was waiting for her with open arms.

"Oh my God, girl, it's been too long!" She embraced Medea and then pushed her back to arms' length, eyeing her up and down. "Jesus, Medea, you look like shit."

"You remember what I said on the radio?" Medea asked. "About the wine?"

"Something about killing a man for a bottle of pinot grigio, I think?"

"Exactly," Medea said. "Go get the damn bottle."

NICHOLAS BRUNER has worked as a carnie, a camp counselor, a construction worker, a swimming pool installer, an assistant for an explosives crew, and a pizza deliverer. He is looking to add novelist to his list of unlikely job titles. He lives in Fairfax, VA with his wife and two children.

A SHORT POEM IN THE SHAPE OF A SWORD BY MICAH BRUNER, MIDDLE SCHOOLER, FOUND BY HIS FATHER, NICK, ON THE KITCHEN TABLE, AND DELIGHTED IN BY THE EDITOR

The
island
is a harsh
place, but if
you are smart
and stay calm
then you may
find a way to
survive and
that way is:
Remember that panic drowns
so
what you need
is to plan, prepare,
prioritize,
practice,
persevere.

STILL LIFE
JOHN H. MATTHEWS

The camera was heavier than I remembered, the silver and black case cold to the touch. I hadn't gotten to hold it often, but it happened a few times under my mother's nervous eyes. When the black limousine pulled up to the house this morning I couldn't get in, not feeling strong enough to sit in such close proximity with my brother with no escape route. He rode in the stretched town car with our two uncles and I drove alone. Hours later, I arrived at the house ahead of everyone else and realized it was the first time I'd been alone there.

It had been three years since I'd even visited, well before my mother's eyesight began to fade from the disease that rapidly overtook her, and my brother wouldn't let me forget it. Now I'm surrounded with her friends and what little family was left, each descending to prove how they loved the old woman most, and expecting to be fed and paid well for that.

The will would not be read for another week, but everyone seemed to know who was getting what. Any money that was left, which wasn't much, would be split between my brother and me and likely a donation to the museum in San Francisco that our mother had loved and that had displayed her work so often. The house would go to my brother. And nobody doubted that the camera in my hands and the rest of the contents of the small studio would be mine soon.

"Already taking inventory?"

"Fuck you, Robbie." My brother picked things up and sat them back down too hard against the wood shelves. "It's not like I asked for any of it."

"Still, you're the one who followed in her footsteps," Robbie said.

"I never did it for her. It was more like I was expected to become a photographer, the only daughter of the famous Vivian Hunter." I punctuated each word as I'd heard it read so many times. "I guess going into advertising was my small way of rebelling against it."

"What are you going to do with all of this junk?" Robbie said.

"I sure don't have room in my apartment," I said. "I'll probably donate some of it to a school or the museum. I'll sell some."

I still held the cold metal camera in my hands, pulled the winding arm back, and pressed the shutter to hear the distinctive clunk of the German made machine. I knew this was one thing I would not sell.

Two weeks later I sat in my small apartment in Brooklyn, surrounded by the boxes that had been shipped from Seattle. The will had been read and everything went as expected. I had packed all of the photography gear up before coming home, knowing Robbie would waste no time in listing our mother's place for sale.

The Leica M3 traveled in my carry-on. It wasn't my mother's newest camera, but it had been her favorite, and the one she'd carried through two decades of documenting.

All of the film in the house had expired, so I'd bought six rolls of black and white slide film at a small camera store in Seattle before departing. The first photo I took with the camera had been with the taxi waiting behind me to go to the airport. I'd held the camera to my face and turned the focus ring on the 50-millimeter lens until the two images aligned in the rangefinder eyepiece, bringing the house into sharp focus, and I'd pressed the shutter.

I knew a few items in these boxes would pay for my rent for the next few years once I found the right buyers or publishers. All of my mother's original negatives were here and were worth far more than the bungalow Robbie inherited, if handled properly. My mother had refused all offers of publishing books of her images, saying they should be seen in grainy newsprint, not in a book.

I hadn't been able to even start sorting through the boxes that were stacked in the corner of my room now. The Leica hadn't left my side, still with only one frame exposed on the roll of thirty-six. During the day I was at work, using the new medium format digital gear that had all but replaced film in the advertising world. At night I sat in my apartment's one window, the camera in my lap like a faithful pet, debating what to photograph next.

Another week went by and the number on top of the camera still pointed at '35'. During lunch I looked up a phone number, dialed and spoke with the man on the other line for a few minutes, setting up a time to meet the next morning.

The sun rose and I was already awake. I showered and dressed, then put the camera in my messenger bag and left the apartment. I took the subway under the river to Manhattan, transferred once, and walked several blocks to the café in Greenwich Village near New York University where the man I was meeting teaches.

"Becca." James Sutton was waiting at the door to the café and greeted me with a hug. "I'm so sorry about your mother. She was one of my dearest friends."

"I know, Mr. Sutton," I said. "She always cared for you."

"It's James, please," he said. "Your mother and I have a long history. Back when she and I started working there were very few professional female photojournalists and even fewer male photographers that would give her the time of day."

We took a table inside with a view of the street and ordered coffee and exchanged more pleasantries.

"So, Becca," James said. "I know you didn't call me to talk just about your mother."

"You're right," I said. "It's about this."

I pulled the camera out of my bag and set it on the table between us.

"Oh my," James said. "She still had it…well, now I guess you have it. You are very lucky, young lady. This camera has seen more than most people would ever hope to in a lifetime."

"And that's my problem," I said. "I loaded it three weeks ago and have taken one photo."

James put the camera back on the table after looking it.

"Your mother did wonderful things," James said. "She pushed boundaries and went places not many people would go, not just women. You can't let that stop you from seeing your own images through the camera."

"I'm an advertising photographer," I said. "I haven't taken pictures outside a studio since my third year of college seven years ago. Mom was in Selma with this camera. She was in Little Rock."

James shook his head and thought, then took a sip of his coffee.

"You can't find yourself not worthy of a camera," James said. "It is a tool, a fine crafted tool, but just a tool. You must make your own art with it. Your mother merely broke it in for you."

I smiled at this thought of thirty years of use being the break in period for the small mechanical device, but it operated now as well as it did when it was brand new.

"How do I start?"

"Start with what you know, then look for what you don't," James said.

I left the café an hour later and took the subway up to Madison Avenue, then walked to my office building. I was late, but nobody noticed or cared as my work was always done ahead of time. I looked at the list of what needed to be photographed and found the schedule boring for the first time. The items I took photos of never excited me, but they had also never bored me before. I was used to looking through her camera at everything from watches to soda cans, small children in clothes sold in stores in every mall in the country and occasionally a minor celebrity. Today it was a new cereal box.

I work alone unless it was a shoot involving live models. I set up the lights and read through all the notes from the art director, then began taking the photos of the box. More than a hundred frames later, I had more than I needed and reviewed the images on the computer screen at my desk.

As I began to take down the lights, I looked at the cereal box and hesitated, then went to my bag and pulled out the old film camera. I walked around the pedestal with the box on it a few times, then framed it in the viewfinder, adjusted the exposure with the dial on top of the body to compensate for the single modeling light that still lit the inanimate object, then took the second exposure on the roll.

The touch of the shutter was satisfying, real. It wasn't like the electronic sounds I got from my work gear. I pulled the arm to wind the film to the next frame and could feel the click of each of the metal cogs on the gear that rotated the spool of 35-millimeter film. I put the lens cap back on and put it in her bag.

The rest of the week went on, and the camera stayed with me. Instead of eating a lunch I'd made from home and carried to work each day, I was leaving the building and exploring a different block of buildings surrounding my workplace. The number on top of the camera gradually decreased. One day, only two images were made, the next day, four.

When the weekend arrived, I woke fresh and excited. I spent Saturday walking around Central Park, then Sunday took the train to Coney Island. I was becoming braver with each click, and in the subjects I would see inside the camera. Inanimate objects gave way to street performers, used to having their picture taken. Then on the boardwalk I saw the other people, the locals and the tourists, the fanny packs and the cross dressers, big tattoos and even bigger hair. I was still being selective, but making progress through my first roll.

When my alarm went off on Monday, I dreaded the idea of going to work. I looked over at the camera and the extra rolls of film sitting on the table. Somehow I found the willpower to clock in and did a lunchtime walk, snapping one new photograph before heading back to the office.

I walked home that evening for the first time since moving to New York. Halfway across the Brooklyn Bridge I turned and looked back at the skyline. The Empire State Building stood majestically on the right, and to the left, the Art Deco Chrysler Building.

Mom had spent time in New York as a photojournalist before having children, but she preferred the small towns with the big issues. I'd spent childhood looking through negatives, slides, and prints from all of Mom's travels, listening to her talk about how I would also go to great places someday.

I slid out he camera and held it to my eye, focused on the mesh of thick support cables that helped keep the bridge up, then rotated the aperture ring to allow more light into the lens while reducing the twin towers to a recognizable blur captured in the spider web pattern of the cables. I pressed the shutter.

My studio apartment felt smaller than usual that night. I'd sat the camera in the middle of the table in front of my small sofa and it became its own centerpiece, pulling they eye towards it whenever you looked in its general direction. It had also become the centerpiece of my waking and sleeping thoughts. It pulled me too.

Later from bed I could see the camera taunting me through the cracked door to the other room, inviting me. I faded to sleep as the images from Mom's negatives floated into my dreams, pulling me into their conversations as if I'd been behind the lens instead of my mother. I saw the Edmund Pettus Bridge as Martin Luther King Jr. led thousands across it. I saw Perry Smith and Richard Hickock hang from lengths of rope in Kansas.

The reality of the events my mother had witnessed turned dreams into nightmares. Before the sun had risen the next day, I had pushed away from the camera in sleep, trying not to see what my mother had seen. I jolted awake with sweat soaked into my pillow and knew I didn't want to go to sleep again. The thought of photographing one more soda can or cereal box repulsed me. For the first time, I felt my mother's blood coarse through my veins.

I showered and chose jeans and a loose fitting blouse, then tied on running shoes. It was certain to get some looks in the elevator and hallways at work, but I wanted to be comfortable to walk back into the city. It was more than a want, or even a need. I desired the walk, craved it, to see the city from the ground.

It was light out once I got to the sidewalk and turned to begin the long walk. I'd removed everything from my bag that wasn't needed in order to lighten the load, reducing the contents to the camera, extra film, my wallet, and an apple for breakfast.

The Leica came out for a moment early on as a dog walked casually down the middle of a side road. I stepped into the street fifty feet ahead of it, found my focus point, adjusted the aperture, and waited a few seconds for the stray to walk into focus. Then I pressed the shutter. As I pulled the lever to wind the film to the next frame, it froze halfway. I'd finished my first roll of film. The dread I had felt for weeks was gone and I quickly changed rolls, eager to begin again.

I reached the Brooklyn end of the bridge and began to cross. Other people walking and biking to work in the city passed me by as I took my time, not caring if I got to work punctually. I stopped to watch as boats cruised under the bridge and spotted the Statue of Liberty, tiny on the horizon.

The beauty of the city began to take shape in front of me. It was something I never saw riding the subway, keeping my head buried in a magazine, avoiding eye contact with the strangers on the train. The skyline spread out from left to right, sun reflected off buildings and the sounds of horns and engines around me more like music than noise pollution. I saw the faces of people walking past into Brooklyn and listened to the quiet clicking of bicycle gears as they rode by.

I reached the halfway point of the bridge where I'd stopped the night before and paused again. In the days I'd been using the old camera, I hadn't taken two of the same shot yet, but the light was different this morning, and I pulled the Leica out of my bag and removed the lens cap.

The camera to my eye, I focused past the mesh of cables this time and brought the towers into clear view in front of me. The 50 millimeter lens provided a wide shot with the towers sharp but small in the middle of the frame, surrounded by the blurred lines, inverse of the shot I'd taken the night before.

I made an aperture adjustment and checked focus again, then took a deep breath and slowly exhaled to steady for the shot.

People nearby stopped, and I thought they were looking to see what I was photographing. I watched my subjects through the viewfinder as the dialogue around me grew louder.

I began to press the shutter as something entered the frame from the right, but the button had traveled too far down. The internal gears took over and the view went dark for one hundredth of a second as the mirror flipped up out of the way of the film plane. The light came through the lens and struck the silver halide crystals to leave a latent image on the negative. The mirror swung back down and the image was made.

As the light came back through the viewfinder, I saw the plane strike the tower as if it were a small movie going on in my eye. I couldn't move while I processed what I was seeing. Someone behind me screamed and I lowered the camera and my brain accepted what it had seen.

I looked around to see time had stopped. Nobody was walking, cars below me on the bridge had come to a standstill and the drivers were beside their vehicles watching to the west.

The weight in my hand called me and I glanced at the top of the camera to see the number on top, 36, staring up at me. The camera had been called into action again, but this time it was me behind it, not my mother. I raised it to my eye and began to frame the onlookers around me. Their faces reflected the lives of the people on that airplane, in that building.

I moved along the bridge. The tragedy of what had happened was growing. Strangers were holding each other, crying, while others just sat and stared at the flames.

A second and a third roll of film were exposed as I shot quickly, moving across the bridge as most people were headed the other direction, off the island. I loaded a fresh roll as I turned the corner to face downtown to the south and raised the camera to my face. Through the viewfinder, I saw the flames from the tower and people standing in the streets around me watching it, still unsure of what had just happened.

The screams came first and grew louder as people on other streets saw what was to happen before I did. The camera didn't leave my eye and I was already focused on the buildings when the second plane came into view.

My mother's negatives flipped through my mind rapidly while I looked up at the burning towers. She saw presidents and royalty, riots and celebrations, life and death. As the mental slideshow faded, I glanced at the camera.

"I understand now."

I pressed the shutter.

THE DAY THE WORLD DID NOT END
ANITA KLEIN

"Who wants to go see the sunrise over the lighthouse!?" Her voice bellows throughout the tiny beach house. Angela walked through the house, turning on all the lights.

I groan into my pillow. *Stop…please…stop screaming.* The room is still dark; it can't possibly be time to wake up yet. I pull the pillow from underneath my head and use it to block out every noise around me.

What time is it? What time did we get back last night? Does she have a snooze button?

More bellowing echoes against the walls. "Hello! It's time to go if you want to see the sunrise!"

Ugh, this was my thing. Sunrise over the lighthouse. I brought us here for this, but my head is pounding and icepicks are stabbing my temples.

Can I just get a sip of water?

"Who wants to see the sunrise?!"

1999 was ending. Much of the world had been preparing for the transition to 2000. Whoever set up the time system on the first computer didn't consider what would happen once 1999 ended. They set up time as a month-month/day-day/year-year format (12/31/99). Not many people used computers when they first came out—who would have ever thought they would run every public system in existence? And who would have thought that the computers would think that what comes after 12/31/99 was 01/01/00, which, in computer time, meant the year 1900? And who would have ever thought that minor oversight could have the potential to wreak havoc on anything that relied on computerized technology?

The whole world feared what might happen.

My plan was to be far, far away from the cities and crowded areas and all those computer glitches just in case every system out there, or even a handful of systems, went haywire.

I couldn't think of a place more removed from the hustle and bustle, a place less reliant on computerized systems, than Ocracoke Island. So long as we got over there before the shit hit the fan, in my mind, we'd be safe. It was perfect, really. New Year's Day fell on a Saturday, so we wouldn't even have to take much time off work to make the trip.

We had gone to Howard's Pub. It truly was our only choice. It boasted OPEN 365 DAYS A YEAR and on this tiny, twelve-mile scrap of island, on New Year's Eve, it was the only open establishment.

We partied.

We sang Prince's "1999" more times than I care to remember.

We rang in the New Year.

I called all of my family to wish them a Happy New Year.

I specifically remember calling my mom, collect, from the bar pay phone (yes, those antiquated things attached to the wall which made the receiver responsible for the charges).

"Happy New Year!" I screamed to her. Calling her at the stroke of midnight had become our tradition. I knew my midnight call always woke her up, but she liked being part of my celebrations, wherever I may be, and that gave us a special bond. We would ring in the New Year via miles of Ma-Bell.

So, to answer the burning question, ME! Me. I want to see the sunrise!

I want to see it come up over the lighthouse. That's why we're here. I'm the one who dragged us out all these miles, in the dead of winter, to this spit of an island, to make sure that we survived in case the world ended. I am the one who wants to see the sunrise.

I force myself out of bed. Throw on some semblance of clothes. I walk into the bathroom, squint at the brightness of the lights, and slowly brush my teeth. I make my way out of the house.

As I walk through the kitchen, I grab a gallon jug of water. Spring water was all we used in the coffee pot; the island water was kind of icky. Thankfully that also meant we always had giant to-go water bottles. I had a feeling we would be craving a lot of water as we waited for the sun to make its appearance. I, for one, had to wash last night's sins from my body. *Will a gallon be enough?*

We had a pretty good idea of the sunrise time. After disembarking the ferry, we drove straight to the island's only convenience store to get the tide chart, which included a sunrise/sunset table.

Angela and I hopped into my rusty Jeep, gallon of water in hand, and slowly made our way through the island roads to the Ocracoke lighthouse. Together, we witnessed the first morning of the year 2000 come into being. We had made it through midnight. Nothing terrible happened. After all of our shenanigans, we survived the night and woke up, alive and well in the year 2000.

I was so thankful that Ang ensured my plan came to fruition. Without her wake-up call, I would have slept through properly welcoming in the new millennium. We passed the jug of water back and forth. We bore witness to the first sunrise of the dreaded Y-2-K.

Once the sun gave enough light to the sky, we bid farewell to the lighthouse, and decided to also welcome the ocean into the New Year. We turned down one of the beach roads, drove over the access ramp, bumped and jostled through the soft sand close to the ramp, and came to a stop on the hard-packed sand near the water's edge. We dipped our toes into the cold waters of the Atlantic. A baptism of an era.

With a small driftwood stick we wrote *January 1, 2000* in the sand and took a picture as proof that the world did not end.

I'm glad it didn't.

My Haiku!!!!

Warm sand underfoot
The ebb and flow of the tide
Serenity mine

A wife, mom, and recent breast cancer survivor, Anita Klein enjoys writing as a means to document and celebrate life's journeys and adventures, both simple and complex. Her blog, F*Cancer, shares her experience with cancer and its treatment, in a voice that is honest, compassionate, funny, and friendly. https://fcancerak.wordpress.com

THE SAND BRIDGE HERO
STEVE MORIARTY

The Duncan family drove the long bridge, crossing over frothing sea water, to begin a week's vacation.

"This place is beautiful, Bill." His wife gazed out the window as they neared the island. "I don't know why you didn't want to come here before now."

Everyone called it Sand Bridge Island, but the real name was forgotten long ago. Its current title came from the original way people reached it.

Situated just off the coast, low tide once exposed a sand bar that served as a temporary passage. Comprised of about two square miles, a rocky shore facing the coast, the island's attraction lay in the long, pristine beach on the ocean side.

The sand was white, easing up to the grass covered dunes that bordered the beach. Local investors, sensing long-term profits, purchased it and installed a permanent bridge, one that would carry vacationers across the water regardless of the tides. Homes were built, each of them rented throughout the summer at exorbitant prices.

Several dozen houses of varying sizes and styles lined the one circular road. They passed a convenience store, the island's only commercial establishment.

"Why do they call it 'The Sand Bridge Hero,' Dad?" asked Kelly, their ten-year-old.

"Maybe it's a sandwich," Ralph, her younger brother replied.

They drove on. The house they'd rented was the last one on the ocean side.

"Everybody out," Bill said when they arrived. "Grab your own stuff and at least one other bag. Don't expect your mother to carry everything."

"'Your mother'?" his wife asked, arching an eyebrow.

"Hey, Dad's all tuckered out," Bill said. "He's been driving for six hours and needs a beer." He piled two bags of groceries on top of the cooler. "But if you insist," he said, and carried them towards the house.

As expected, the children wanted to get to the beach as soon as possible. "Sunscreen on, and no one goes down to the water without Dad," their mother said. "I'll fix lunch."

Bill walked behind the older two and held the youngest by the hand. The waves were low, barely rippling onto the shore. A light breeze drifted inward. He lifted and carried Esther, holding her close as he slowly waded into the ocean. The little girl laughed, slapping at the water as it rose and fell, and shrieked with delight each time it reached her. Kelly and Ralph played in the shallows.

After about half an hour they returned to the house, where lunch was ready. *Maybe they'll take a nap afterward,* Bill thought. *And Louise and I can spend a few moments on the beach together.*

"Bill," she said, "can you run up to the store for a gallon of milk? That's the one thing we didn't bring."

"Not likely," he muttered, knowing how they always forgot telephones, maps, medicines and other essentials.

"Pardon me?"

"I said, 'I'd like that.'"

He slipped into a pair of sandals and went back up the road to the store.

The Sand Bridge Hero offered all of the beach basics: the food selection one would expect at a 7-Eleven, sun tan lotion, beach towels, blow-up rafts and Styrofoam coolers. Behind the counter was a young man, apparently in his teens, with long sun-bleached hair and an earring. Bill went to the refrigerator and picked out the carton of milk with the best expiration date and a six-pack of beer. *Louise will need this,* he chuckled to himself.

He put the items on the counter and the boy rang them up. "If you get a twelve-pack it works out cheaper, y'know," he said.

"I'll come back," Bill said, then asked, "say, what's the name of this place mean?"

The boy gave him a blank look.

"The store."

"Oh," the boy said. "I thought maybe you meant the island. You don't know the story?"

My own children might grow up to be morons, Bill thought. *I should be patient.*

"Right. I'm from out of town and don't know the story. What is it?"

"Oh, man. Everybody around here knows it. Local folklore. It happened about twenty-five years ago. There was this guy. He rescued three girls. Swam about a mile with one of them on his back."

"A mile?" Bill said. "That's a long way in the ocean."

"Yeah. There was a real bad storm down the coast. Big waves hitting the island, bad undertow and everything. Them girls got in trouble, and he just went out and got two of them, but by the time he had to go after the third one she was way the hell out there." He laughed, shaking his head, waving blonde tendrils about his face. "I mean *way* the hell out there."

"It sounds like you were on the beach watching."

"Nah. I wasn't even born yet. But my dad was. He told me about it lots of times. Everybody on the island saw it."

Bill nodded. "So, who was this guy?"

"I don't know his name. I don't think anyone does, now. He like, y'know, was just here on vacation and, y'know, saved them girls. I heard later on he tried out for the Olympics."

Bill nodded again. "How'd he do?"

The kid shook his head, his hair twisting around like a yellow tornado. "Don't know, man, but he was a stud I hear. About six-foot-five, big sucker. Must've been a monster. And so, that's where the name for this place comes from."

"The guy was definitely a stud," Bill said.

He thanked the boy, paid for the milk and beer, and left. He walked back to his family's house, stopping in front of a gray bungalow. One story, wide front veranda with a screened porch in back. It sat empty.

It seems smaller than I remember, he thought.

* * *

The young man dated Brenda during his junior year of college. She invited him to the beach the following summer.

Her parents rented a house, and she took a chance on showing off her new boyfriend.

It was August, hot as blazes, and his construction job for the summer was over. His senior year beckoned and he figured that Brenda wanted to be a part of it. He liked that idea.

The house was a bungalow, right across the street from the beach. Brenda's parents, he learned, liked the beach but not the water. They would spend most of their vacation on the veranda, watching the ocean and drinking bourbon.

The first day, right after breakfast, he and Brenda crossed the street bearing all the necessities: blanket, cooler, books, Coppertone, and unrestrained youth. A stiff wind was blowing from inland, kicking up sand. The sky was clear, but a storm down the coast stirred up the water, making it unusually rough. Waves crashed on the beach, swells and whitecaps surged beyond the breakers, and a strong undertow made swimming hazardous, if not impossible. They barely got in the water before retreating to their blanket.

An hour was enough for Brenda.

"Let's go to the house," she suggested. "We can come back later if we want."

He picked up all of the accoutrements again and lugged them across the street. Brenda's mother – always the consummate hostess – fixed sandwiches. They sat on the screened porch, talked and played cards for the next few hours, interrupted only when Brenda's father brought a round of drinks.

"You like gin gimlets?" he asked.

"Never heard of them," the young man said.

"You'll like this one."

He did.

Her father seems to like me, too, he thought. *Maybe he thinks I'll put up with his daughter's unpredictable but entertaining antics.*

Around 5:00 that evening Brenda's mother stepped onto the porch.

"Why don't you two go down to the water one more time while I finish up dinner?" she said. "It'll be ready when you get back."

They put on their swimsuits again. The evening sun was low in the sky and the wind reduced to a mild breeze. But the water was still as rough as earlier in the day. They waded out near the breakers, holding hands to steady each other, the surging waves cresting against them.

Brenda wore an orange bikini, thoughtfully chosen, he figured, to show off that fine figure of hers. *They can't make those things any smaller,* he thought. *Her circulation will be cut off.* She laughed and held him, playfully brushing against his chest.

I might just take her to Homecoming this fall, he thought. *Pretty good way to start the year.*

His amorous thoughts were interrupted by a cry for help. He looked outward as about ten yards away two girls floated past. They cried out again.

"Are they serious?" Brenda asked. "They aren't that far out."

"They're just kidding," he said.

The girls called to them once more.

"Are you alright?" he shouted.

"No!" one of them responded. "We can't get in!"

They'd been swept into deeper water, over their heads. The undertow was too strong, he realized, and they were being pulled out to sea.

"Pick one," he said to Brenda. "Let's go get 'em."

"Are you sure?" she said.

"You're a lifeguard, right?"

"But only in a neighborhood pool."

"I don't think they'll mind."

They dove through the breakers and swam to the girls.

He got to one and reached under her arm, pulling her to his side.

"We'll be okay," he told her. "I'll get you in." Mimicking what he'd seen on television, he put one arm over her shoulder and across her chest and began to swim towards the shore. The waves tangled their legs.

"Hold on," he told her, rearranging their positions. "Get on my back."

He tried breaststroke, getting as near to horizontal in the water as possible, hoping to crest above the undertow. Staying on the surface, they were soon inside the breakers and on sand.

He lifted her off his back and carried her up the beach, depositing her onto dry land, then turned to see how Brenda was doing with the other one.

Stunned, he saw her alone, swimming towards the shore. The other girl was by then at least fifty yards beyond the breakers, barely visible among the waves. He ran into the water, meeting Brenda as she staggered to safety.

"What's going on?" he asked.

She coughed and spat. "She panicked. She'd have drowned the both of us. I had to let her go."

Let her go? he thought. *Who's going to get her now?* He looked up and down the beach. No one. He looked back at Brenda. He turned to the water and saw the girl's head bobbing between white caps, drifting out into the sea. *She's getting farther away every moment.*

"Dammit," he said, and dove back into the water.

He swam towards where he'd last seen the girl. The incoming waves slapped his face as he tried to breathe between strokes. *It's like climbing mountains of water,* he thought. He stopped and looked around, trying to find her. *Maybe a boat will come along.*

There were no boats. He spotted a brief flash of her, disappearing again behind the rising and falling waves. He pressed on.

Maybe it's too late, he thought. *Maybe she's already gone. I should turn back. It's too far. I'll never get us both in.*

He saw her again, a few strokes away, and swam to her.

She was exhausted when he reached her. She'd been crying, he could tell. *Praying, too, no doubt.*

"I've got you," he said. "Hang onto me. We'll be alright." She nodded, coughing. He put her on his back and looked to the shore, surprised at how far away it was.

I've never been this far out before. The beach looks like a thin ribbon. I can't even see any people. Where the hell is Brenda?

He swam. And swam. After a while he looked up and over the waves to check their progress.

My God, he thought, his heart sinking. *We've lost ground.*

We're going out to sea.

The waves rolled over them, relentless.

So this is how it ends.

He stopped, the girl still hanging on his back. *I can just see tomorrow's paper:* SWIMMER, 21, DIES IN FAILED RESCUE ATTEMPT.

The waves lifted, then pushed them down, rolling over their heads. Over and over.

He treaded water, resting, rising and falling with the surging waves. The sky began to darken.

And she'll die, too. Dammit.

He turned around and looked at her. *Then I guess I can't quit.*

"Lie flat," he told her. "Put your arms out in front and keep them there. Whatever happens, stay on top of the water."

He slipped beneath her, grabbed her hips, and kicked. And kicked. And kicked.

If I quit we'll both drown. But if I keep going at least there's a chance. We might not make it, but if my legs don't give out ...

The waves rolled on. About two feet beneath the surface, he noted, the undertow was roaring out to sea. The waves rushed over them, but still moved towards the beach.

Just stay on top.

As they rose and fell between the surges he popped his head up to breathe, then went back beneath the girl and kicked against the roiling water. And kicked.

He looked ahead during one breath. The beach was a little closer. *There's a chance. At least we're going in the right direction.*

His labor continued. Hips and thighs ached, shoulders strained, but he held the girl above him.

Well, I know what happens if I stop. He glanced ahead again. Over the waves he could see that a small crowd had gathered. A man was standing knee-deep in the water, signaling with his hands as if to say, "This way."

He snorted. *Knowing the direction to go ain't my problem right now.*

The surging of the waves increased as they neared the shore. His knees scraped against the bottom.

They rolled through the breakers and crashed into the sand.

The older man ran to them, snatched up the girl, and carried her away. The young man rested on his hands and knees, still in the surf. His lungs swelled and heaved, water surging over his back. He crawled, collapsing on the beach.

Brenda sat next to him.

"You okay?" she whispered and put her hand on his back.

He tried to speak but no words came.

"You saved her," she said. "That was fantastic. You were ..."

His breathing slowed, his lungs rasping.

"Just ... let me ... lie here ... a while."

The crowd stood around him. He heard an unfamiliar voice.

"Nice goin', fella. Ain't nobody was gonna get that girl back in. Thems are some bad waves. That girl was a goner for sure."

Brenda said something but he heard nothing more. *I didn't think we'd get in. I thought it was over.* Her mother arrived. He overheard someone describe something that vaguely resembled what happened.

"What can I do?" she asked.

"A … gin … gimlet," he whispered.

After a few minutes they helped him up, Brenda and her mother each putting one of his arms over their shoulders, then walked back across the street.

"You're a lot heavier than you look, for a skinny fella," the mother said.

He nodded, saying nothing.

"Well, dinner's ready," she said.

They reached the front door.

"I'm covered with sand," he said. "Let me shower off first."

The women went through the front door. He went around back to the outdoor stall, entered, latched the door, peeled off his suit, and let the water run over him. He closed his eyes, envisioning the disappearing shoreline and the little girl's face.

I almost turned around. I almost let her go.

He sank to the floor of the shower, naked, and wept.

What would I have said to her parents, if they knew I'd failed her?

"Are you almost ready?" Brenda's mother called from the porch. "Dinner's on."

Would I have said I'm sorry, I was afraid?

He stood, his hands pressed against the stall on either side of the shower nozzle.

"Almost done," he said. "Just another minute." He put his face in the warm spray, washing away his tears.

He went to his room where he dressed, combed his hair

and checked his reflection. Sunburned, red eyes, but alive. And hungry.

"Well," the mother announced when they all were seated. "I think someone should give you a medal."

"Someone," the father said, lifting his glass. "A medal."

Brenda was next to him, her hand beneath the table on his thigh.

"You were the hero today," she said, stroking him. "My hero."

I wouldn't have had to be, if you hadn't quit on that second one.

"Care for some wine?" Brenda's father offered.

"Fill 'er up," he said, reaching with his glass.

"How far did you have to swim with that girl, anyway?" the father asked.

He thought a moment. "Maybe seventy-five yards. Maybe a little less. It was hard to tell. It felt like a mile."

"It had to be at least a mile," Brenda beamed. "At least."

The women continued to talk about the event from every perspective, over and over. The young man busied himself with corn on the cob, grilled chicken, and several glasses of wine.

After dinner they sat in the living room. Someone came to the front door.

Brenda's mother let in a woman, followed by two young girls, freshly showered and looking embarrassed.

"Say it," the woman said.

"Thank you," the girls mumbled. "Thank you for rescuing us."

"We were so upset, me and my husband," the woman began, softly. "No one remembered their manners." Turning to the girls, "These are my daughters."

They were twelve and fourteen, she explained, and had no idea what an undertow was. They'd run down to the beach just after arriving and ahead of their parents.

He looked at them. They were all angles, braces, and long hair, reminding him of young colts. Awkward, perhaps, but just a glance at them and he knew they'd be pretty and graceful when they were older.

"Their dad and I didn't know the water was so bad, and when he got down there, well, … my girl …" She started to cry. "My little girl … oh, my goodness."

The woman put her face in her hands and sobbed as Brenda's mother embraced her. "There, now, honey. It's alright now. Alright now." She patted the woman on her back gently. "It's alright and your little babies are just fine."

The girls stared at their feet. Brenda put her arm around him.

After a moment the woman reached for his hand. He was embarrassed and said nothing. "You're my family's savior," she said, softly, wiping away her tears. "You saved us. All of us."

I was no hero, he thought. *I looked up and down that damned beach for someone else to go after her. Wasn't anybody else there but me.*

He shook his head.

"Thanks, ma'am," was all he could manage, choking on the words. "I'm just glad we got in."

The woman then turned to Brenda. "Are you two, you know, together?"

"Oh, yes," she said, circling her arm around his and

snuggling her head against his shoulder. "He's my boyfriend."

His stomach tightened and he started to speak, but Brenda continued.

"He's something, isn't he? He's going to get a medal."

"A medal," said Brenda's father, nodding.

The woman and her daughters departed, night fell, and Brenda's parents drifted off to bed.

"Care for a walk on the beach, hero man?" Brenda suggested.

They held hands as they walked through the ebbing foam. The crashing waves of earlier in the day had subsided. The water was nearly flat, a dark mirror reflecting the moonlight.

She held him and smiled. "You were really something today. Want to try for that swim now?"

The beach was deserted, lit only by the stars and the moon. She pulled off her sweatshirt, revealing a different bikini.

"C'mon," she said.

"I think I've had enough of the ocean for one day," he said.

"C'mon," she purred.

Stepping back, she unhooked her swim suit top and tossed it to him.

"I'm going in," she said, and tiptoed into the water.

He stood on the beach watching her silhouette in the moonlight as she turned and dove into the darkness. She surfaced, waving the bottom of her suit over her head then throwing it to the shore. She pulled back her wet hair.

"What are you waiting for, an engraved invitation?" she called to him with a laugh as she dove again.

He unbuttoned his shirt, then dropped to his knees. His hands reached out in front of him, digging into the sand.

I almost let her go.

* * * *

The children went down for naps, and just as Bill had hoped, the long drive, brief time in the water and lunch had taken their toll.

"Let's take a swim," Louise said. "This is our vacation, too."

"Sounds good to me," he said, and they quietly slipped out the door.

"You took a long time at the store," she said as they walked, holding hands.

"Just talking to a local guy."

"Anything interesting?"

"Nah. Regular stuff."

The beach was quiet, the only sounds the rhythmic sloshing of the surf and the squawking of seagulls. He squeezed her hand gently, looked into her eyes and smiled.

Everything I could have wanted.

"I want to swim," she said. "C'mon."

Louise walked into the water gingerly, turning to him.

"It's cold, but feels great. Aren't you coming?"

"I'll be along," he said.

He watched her dip into the waves, rise up and push back her wet hair, smile and wave to him, then swim out to deeper water. He thought of Kelly, Ralph, and Esther. Little Esther.

Will someone be there for her one day?

"Hey, are you coming? It's wonderful," Louise called to him.

Will I get a call? "Your child is gone," someone might say. *"No one could get to her."*

He slowly knelt, leaning forward on his hands, his fingers clutched.

I almost let her go. Tears ran down the bridge of his nose, dropping to the sand. *My God, I almost let her go.*

STEVE MORIARTY grew up in Falls Church and has lived in Northern Virginia all his life. He is married with four children, and when not writing, running or repairing his house he practices a little law.

THE TRANSCRIBER CHRONICLES THE FOLLOWING RECORDING ON THE DEVICE RECOVERED AT THE COORDINATES -17.6417°, 179.8323°, 17:50 HOURS, MAY 9TH, 2019.

S.C. MEGALE

I suppose you want to know why I jumped from a plane at twelve thousand feet without a parachute.

This thing is on, right?

Yes, well, don't mind the wind. The mic was cheap, and it isn't like I'd be able to write a note now.

It'll be another forty seconds or so until I die. I'm not sure that's time to explain.

Dreadful. You're all dreadful. Is that enough?

Oh, what the hell - it began probably with Porty. You'll find him in a UPS box at the Levuka Orphanage, right next to Pirate Cove Resort, because he doesn't get along well with other birds.

See I bought Porty from a native who'd worn an iguana around his neck and a straw hat with the strands fanning out like a porcupine. He sneezed on my money, wiped his nose, and handed over the African grey. Porty was fat, downy, and with eyes that pulsed open and closed like a camera shutter. I do swear I loved him.

I – good Lord, I have to shout for you to hear this – I STUCK PORTY IN –

The transcriber notes an increase in volume

– a white cage and we ate fried plantains while staring at each other through the bars until he suddenly blurt "Treasure on the island!"

I remember distinctly the *clank!* of my fork hitting the bowl and I asked him to clarify what treasure, what island?

"Treasure on the island!" Porty squawked. "Horseshoe!"

Upon reflection he might have been mimicking the native's "Achoo!" but I heard "horseshoe" and my front door slammed and Porty's cage rattled as I took off a second later. Bowl broken on the floor.

There is a raspberry - the speaker spitting hair out of his face? Inconclusive

I been on island hoppers, okay?! I know I'd seen an acre-large island in horseshoe shape beneath the yellow wings of the plane once. You know what the locals said when I asked them back on earth? NOTHING! They pretended they didn't know what I spoke of.

Porty knew.

Every night, the endless echo…

"Treasure on the island! Horseshoe!"

HOW MANY TIMES? How many times did I groan and fold the pillow over my ears?!

"Treasure on the island! Horseshoe!"

Ten years of my life - TEN YEARS! - I have whacked palms with my machete, Porty on my shoulder. "Here, Porty?! Is this the spot?!" Kicking aside dirt and climbing the creaking mast of a sailboat to lift binoculars to my eyes. I have ripped down books and spent thousands on expeditions to find that island again. We've discovered SIXTY-SEVEN in the Pacific, and none a horseshoe.

They laugh at me, this world of idiots.

Transcriber notes either a laugh or a sob. Twice rewound it is hard to conclude

I was fired, they took visiting rights with the kids away. I was put on "watch." *Insane*, they said.

Porty knows. Porty knows I'm not insane.

Ask him, dammit! Levuka Orphange, 2900 Beach Street!

Everyone cruel to me! Everyone whispering. In all my life here in Fiji I have learned humans are no better than fish, and I'd rather die with fish now that I've lost all at the hands of humans and birds. I'd rather -

The transcriber notes a ruffling, scratching sound and then steady wind

SHIT! DAMMIT! CAN YOU HEAR ME? I DROPPED THE RECORDER, BUT IT'S FALLING AT MY SIDE. I'LL YELL MY LAST WORDS.

YOU DID THIS, PORTY! YOU LIED TO ME AND DROVE ME MAD. IT'S TRUE! YOU KNEW YOU WOULD! YOU WANTEDTHIS!

TREASURE ON THE ISLAND!

HORSESOE!

AND NOW I'M DEAD! MAY THEY PLUCK EVERY FEATHER FROM YOUR FAT PARROT ASS! I SPENT MY LAST COIN ON A SKYDIVE AND MY LAST WORDS ON A LIE BECAUSE OF YOU!

KILL THAT BIRD AS MY LAST WISH!

2900 BEACH STREET!

2900 BEACH STEEET!

2900–!

The transcriber notes a pause of about two seconds

WHAT?

Indistinguishable

WHAT IS THAT? THAT'S NOT – THAT'S NOT WATER.

PORTY. PORTY! IT CAN'T BE! PORTY, IT'S– *PORTY! IT'S RE–!*

The transcriber notes a very loud series of muffles, cracks, and thumps. The recording screeches once and terminates.

USS HUMANITY
DAWN VAN DYKE

Twenty-three damn days. That's how long I've been here on this godforsaken island. Each day that humanity sails by me without a glance, my hope for rescue is a little harder to hold.

Twenty-one days ago, I pretended being beached here wasn't so bad. Warm fingers of the sun caress my face in the morning. The salt on my skin is sharp and harsh like the ocean. The breeze is steady. There is a monotonous whoosh of lapping, but this is not Tortuga.

In movies, when someone is stranded on an island, they just wave their arms for help and they get rescued.

I tried that.

I heard the gears shift faster and saw the eyes shift to... to where? How can you look anywhere else when I'm hopping up and down, waving like the mad person I am becoming?

I'm atrophying – body, mind, and soul.

Maybe I've become a ghost. That might explain why people don't see me and, yet, avoid shipwrecking too. But ghosts don't get sunburned. Ghosts don't get thirsty.

I am not the only one haunting this island, hoping for humanity to notice me. Many have shipwrecked here before and, I am sure, many more will come. Some simply lose their way. Some didn't have enough support crew for the journey. Some are running away from something.

Some just plain ran out of money; addiction or medical bills, it doesn't matter. When you're out, you're out. And when you're out, you crash here with the other lost souls of Washington Circle.

Before I was stranded here, I had a decrepit little apartment with broken window panes on Southside. God, that seems like a castle now. Drafty and dark in the winter. A man's house is his castle. Sounds like some BS you'd see on a pillow, tucked in right next to HOME IS WHERE THE HEART IS. That's the kind of crap my mom used to buy when I was a kid. My heart is in Washington Circle now and it sure as shit isn't home. It is home-less. I am homeless... for now.

I have to remember: this is temporary. Twenty-three days temporary, but still temporary. I see the others in this camp with their bags of treasured trash covered in pigeon crap feeding the city seagulls. They've given up. They've started to build a home here. Not me.

I am going to get off this island.

Dawn Van Dyke has more than a decade of experience writing pithy taglines and news releases across diverse industries, including healthcare, e-commerce, non-profits, and associations. She joined The Writers of Chantilly this year to hone her craft, unlearn AP Style, and eventually write more than six hundred words at a time.